"Mom?" he said in a sleepy tone, having just woken up, too. "Do you smell smoke? I thought maybe I was dreaming about Dad."

"It's not a dream, Josh." Her heart squeezed for her son, who obviously missed his father. Sam had died only seven months ago, and so much had happened since then, not least of all the recent move to this house. She could understand why he'd made the connection. When her firefighter husband had been alive, he'd often come home reeking of smoke. It was the same smell filling the air now. "Come here." She reached out and gathered him in a one-armed hug. "Let's see what's going on."

In the living room, red and blue lights flashed brightly through the front window. Screaming fire trucks pulled up, too, blocking the end of their driveway. Pressing her nose against the glass, she peered out and saw firefighters and police gathering around the house next door, the Tollivers' place. There hadn't been time to get close to her neighbors, but she had briefly met single mom Anna Tolliver and her two girls, who were both a few years younger than Josh.

"Wow," Josh whispered beside her. Now that he realized their house wasn't the one on fire, he relaxed a little. "I've never seen a fire this close."

"Me neither," Lindsey admitted. As an ED nurse working in a small community hospital, she'd been exposed to the occasional burns patient, but nothing really serious. All the really serious cases had been airlifted to Los Angeles.

She shivered, despite the warmth of the balmy California spring night.

A firefighter dressed in full gear jogged across her front lawn, heading to her front door. She pulled back in surprise, and then opened the door before he had a chance to knock.

"Lindsey?" Her husband's best friend and fellow firefighter and paramedic, Austin Monroe, gaped at her in shock. "What in the devil are you doing here?"

Great. Just what she needed. Not. She stifled a sigh and angled her chin, fervently wishing

When they finally had the fire under control he helped stow the gear, his gaze searching for Lindsey and little Josh. There was no way he was going to allow them to return to their place.

"Lindsey?" He made his way over to where she and Josh both stood, looking a bit shell-shocked, their arms wrapped around each other for support. "I'll take you over to my place for what's left of the night, okay?"

"A hotel is fine. We don't need to impose."

"You're not imposing." Just once, he wished she'd simply give in and let him help. "You can stay with me for as long as you need to," he said in a low tone.

She was so beautiful, even with her long blond hair mussed and not a speck of make-up on her face. He had a hard time tearing his gaze from her profile.

Knock it off, Monroe, he warned himself. Stop thinking of Lindsey as a woman you're attracted to. He'd promised to take care of them. Lindsey needed a friend right now. A helping hand. A shoulder to lean on.

Not a man who fantasized about being more.

Dear Reader

Isn't it amazing to discover how Mills & Boon is celebrating its centennial birthday? One hundred years of publishing romance. I'm honoured to be writing for the Mills & Boon family, since I began reading Harlequin romances well over thirty years ago. As a teenager I found hope and comfort in romance, and even today, as a critical care nurse, I'm all too aware of the sadness and realism in the world. I very much prefer a happy ending, where strength and true love always prevail.

I'm thrilled to be a part of making history with this book, THE FIREFIGHTER AND THE SINGLE MUM. This is the fourth book in the Monroe Family series. When firefighter Austin Monroe discovers his best friend's widow Lindsey Winters and her son Josh have fallen on difficult times, he feels he must step in to help. Lindsey prefers to remain independent, but she can't deny her son the male guiding hand he desperately needs. Austin has a reputation for being a playboy, but is it possible that Austin's love 'em and leave 'em attitude hides a deep, unrequited love for Lindsey?

I hope you enjoy Austin and Lindsey's story. Thanks so much for choosing to celebrate one hundred years of romance with Mills & Boon.

Sincerely

Laura Iding

THE FIREFIGHTER AND THE SINGLE MUM

BY
LAURA IDING

MILLS & BOON
Pure reading pleasure™

First published in Great Britain 2008
Large Print edition 2008
Harlequin Mills & Boon Limited,
Eton House, 18-24 Paradise Road,
Richmond, Surrey TW9 1SR

© Laura Iding 2008

ISBN: 978 0 263 19978 9

Set in Times Roman 16½ on 20 pt.
17-0908-45444

Printed and bound in Great Britain
by Antony Rowe Ltd, Chippenham, Wiltshire

Laura Iding loved reading as a child, and when she ran out of books she readily made up her own, completing a little detective mini-series when she was twelve. But, despite her aspirations for being an author, her parents insisted she look into a 'real' career. So the summer after she turned thirteen she volunteered as a Candy Striper and fell in love with nursing. Now, after twenty years of experience in trauma/critical care, she's thrilled to combine her career and her hobby into one—writing Medical™ Romances for Mills & Boon. Laura lives in the northern part of the United States, and spends all her spare time with her two teenage kids (help!)—a daughter and a son—and her husband. Enjoy!

Recent titles by the same author:

BABY: FOUND AT CHRISTMAS
BRIDE FOR A SINGLE DAD
HIS PREGNANT NURSE
THE DOCTOR'S CHRISTMAS PROPOSAL

This book is dedicated to my friend
and fellow author, Beth Watson.
Thanks for always being there
when I need someone to talk to.

PROLOGUE

"HEAD for the river, dammit. *Run!*"

Austin Monroe could barely hear Sam's voice over the roar of the wildfire bearing down on them. He didn't need his buddy's urging to keep him moving—the heat of the fire scorching his back was motivation enough. The wind had shifted, bringing the fire they'd been fighting straight toward them, breaking through the line. If not for Sam coming back to warn him, he would have been sunk.

They still might die.

Even as the thought formed, Austin caught sight of the river less than fifty yards ahead. Reaching the river before the fire caught up to them was their only chance of survival.

A slim chance, if the severe drought hadn't made the river too low.

The heavy Kevlar suit he wore wasn't enough to keep the force of the heat off him. He ignored the sweat rolling into his eyes beneath the helmet as he stayed focused on the river.

He slipped, nearly fell, but Sam was right behind him, dragging him upright and pushing him forward. With a Herculean effort, he made his way down the bank to the water, jumping in with a feeling of relief, dousing his whole body as best he could in water that was only knee-high.

It took him a minute to realize Sam hadn't joined him in the river. He glanced back to see his partner using a drip torch to light a backfire on the grassy area surrounding the riverbank to protect them from a lethal burn-over.

He pulled himself back out of the water to join Sam. They didn't have much time as the wildfire bore down on them, moving with astronomical speed as it gobbled up the dry brush with voracious hunger.

"Get into the river!" Sam shouted, lighting as many fires as he could with the drip torch. Austin had lost his equipment when the fire had changed direction, so he couldn't do much to help.

"No." He wasn't leaving his partner, the guy who'd come back for him, to face this alone. When the drip torch was empty, Sam tossed it into the smoldering grass fire. Austin grabbed Sam's arm. "Let's go. We have to get into the water."

This time Sam didn't argue, but finally followed him back down the bank to the river. When Austin hit the water, he felt Sam fall heavily onto him from behind, pinning him down. Austin reached up and pulled Sam down into the water beside him.

The backfire didn't work as well as they'd hoped, and orange flames flickered dangerously close. Following Sam's lead, Austin ripped off his helmet and took a big gulp of air, before submerging his whole head in the water. He sensed Sam did the same, although the smoke was so thick it was hard to see.

Over and over again, he quickly lifted his head, gasped for what little oxygen was left in the air and then ducked his head beneath the water again.

Finally the roar subsided, indicating the fire had burned down, the raging beast having moved on to better prey—thick brush lining the ridge to the west of them.

"Sam?" Austin levered himself to his hands and knees, reaching for his friend. Sam's smoke-blackened face peered up at him and his heart squeezed in his chest. Hadn't Sam continued dunking his head beneath the water? "Are you all right?"

Sam gave a tiny nod, but his breathing was harsh, labored. Austin reached for his radio, wondering just how much smoke had gotten into his buddy's lungs. "Mayday, mayday. Firefighter with smoke inhalation is down in the Rock River, two miles east of the river's bend. Need medic stat."

"Roger that. Medevac chopper on the way."

"Sam?" Panic clawed up his back as Sam began to cough, his body convulsing so hard he could barely take a breath. "Hang on, they're coming for us, buddy, just hang on."

"Lindsey." Sam reached up and grasped Austin's jacket. "Take care of her for me. Take care of Lindsey and Josh."

Sam's plea for his wife and child stabbed his heart. His gut clenched with fear. "Don't worry about Lindsey and Josh. You're gonna make it out of here to take care of them yourself."

"Too late," Sam whispered between coughing fits. "Take care of them—promise me. They'll need... Promise me..." His voice faded as another coughing fit seized him.

"I promise." Austin held his partner close, scanning the smoke-darkened sky. Where in the hell was that chopper?

Sam stopped coughing, closed his eyes and slumped bonelessly in Austin's arms. No. No! He stared down at his buddy, as the medevac chopper cleared the trees and headed for them, knowing with a sick certainty that Sam had been right.

It was too late.

CHAPTER ONE

SMOKE. Accompanied by the wail of sirens.

Lindsey Winters was used to the sirens—they blared past her house often in this part of the city—but it was the acrid smell of smoke that forced her to climb out of her sofa bed located in the center of her living room.

A quick glance around showed nothing amiss. The living room and kitchen were essentially one room and she hadn't left a candle burning, or any other obvious source of smoke. One nice thing about having a small house was that there weren't too many places to look for a fire.

She hastily pulled on a robe and headed down the hall to the single bedroom toward the back of the cottage, where her nine-year-old son slept. "Josh?"

that out of all the firefighters in Sun Valley, Austin Monroe hadn't been on duty tonight. "I live here."

"What? Since when?" he demanded. Then he gave an impatient shake of his head. "Never mind. Come on, we need you and Josh to evacuate the premises. The fire is too close and too far out of control to ensure your safety."

"Is there time for us to change our clothes?" she asked, rubbing one bare foot over the other.

Austin frowned, glancing down at her bare toes and then at her son's equally bare feet. "Two minutes. If you're not ready by then, I'm coming in after you."

No need for threats—she believed him. Turning away from the door, she gave Josh a slight push. "Get dressed. Hurry." As he disappeared down the hall, she grabbed the closest pair of jeans, a sweater, socks and comfortable running shoes she could find and ducked into the bathroom to change.

In less than two minutes she met Josh and

headed outside, resisting the urge to gather her meager yet precious belongings. Through the mass of people milling about she saw Anna Tolliver and her girls standing off to the side, surrounded by police. Thank heavens they were safe.

Austin noticed them when they stepped out onto the porch and crossed over. He directed them to a spot safely beyond the perimeter of the fire. "I need both of you to stand back here, out of the way."

Again, she wasn't going to argue. Austin had been her husband's smoke jumping partner and he knew his way around fires, whether they were the domestic sort like at the Tollivers' house or a thick, raging wildfire. Smoke jumpers were men who fought wildfires by jumping from planes into smoke-filled skies to help prevent the fire from spreading. Her husband and Austin had both trained as smoke jumpers. She'd thought they'd been nuts.

Now she was grateful for Austin's experience in fighting fires.

From their safety zone Lindsey could see orange flames dancing out of the kitchen window of the Tollivers' house. She swallowed hard when she realized how close the threat was to her cottage. Flames reached up, like gnarled fingers trying to grasp the edge of her roof. The postage-stamp-sized lots on which their cottages were built only gave a couple of feet of clearance between them.

"Lindsey?" Austin lightly grasped her arm.

She tore her gaze from the horrifying image of the flames leaping toward her home. "What?"

"Don't leave without me, OK? I'll take care of you and Josh. Just wait for me."

Her throat was clogged with fear so she simply nodded. No matter how annoyed she may have been with him earlier, right now it was nice to know she wasn't totally alone in the world. Austin may be a bit of an interfering control freak, but he was definitely a man of his word. Her gaze followed him as he turned and jogged back, taking his role in fighting the fire. She wanted to watch him work, but quickly lost him amidst the sea of firefighters, unable to distinguish him from the others beneath the heavy gear.

"Mom?" Josh asked, in a tiny, scared voice. "Is our house gonna burn, too?"

She clutched him close, wishing she could sound positive when she had a sinking feeling that things were about to go from bad to worse. After Sam had died, she'd discovered a mountain of debt. She'd been forced to sell the house, grasping the first meager offer that had come in, and had moved here, into this tiny one-bedroom cottage in a not-so-nice part of town.

This probably wasn't the time to admit she had absolutely no insurance. Heck, they'd only moved in two months ago. It had been hard enough to make sure there had been money for food and gas, much less for home owner's insurance.

"I hope not, Josh," she said, watching the flames of her neighbor's house dance closer. The firefighters aimed a wide, forceful stream of water directly toward the source of the fire, completely drenching her house in the process.

She knew she should be glad they were all OK, but what would happen if their house did catch fire? Where would they go? Where would they live?

She blinked away tears of useless self-pity. "I really hope not."

Still reeling from the shock of finding Lindsey and Josh in the tiny, cramped house on Puckett Street, Austin concentrated on fighting the fire. Thankfully, the occupants of the house had gotten out safely, but the fire, having somehow started in the electrical system inside the walls, had traveled along the electrical wires, engulfing the entire place before anyone had even realized what had happened.

The house was a total loss. The goal now was to contain the fire, hopefully preventing it from spreading to the homes on either side.

Particularly to Lindsey's house.

Damn, he wondered what in the heck had happened. Why on earth had she moved out of the nice place she'd lived in with Sam? Because of the memories? Or for financial reasons? As much as he'd tried to be there for Lindsey, especially during those first few weeks after Sam's death, she'd resisted his support. In fact, they'd had a huge fight when he'd tried to give her some advice on how to handle Josh. She'd shouted at him to get a life of his own and to leave her alone.

He'd backed off, giving her the space she'd needed. He hadn't been to see her in five months. First he'd headed off to a smoke jumping tour, being dropped via parachute into the depths of the Oregon forest to fight a wildfire burning out of control, and then, when he'd gotten back, he'd gone home to visit his parents, haunted by memories of Sam the whole time he had been in Oregon.

But he'd failed Sam again, because things were obviously worse for Lindsey than he'd realized. She'd kicked him out of her life once, but he shouldn't have left. He'd assumed she had at least been happily settled in her home. He never wanted to hurt her, but this time he wasn't leaving her alone until he knew she and Josh were safe and secure.

And preferably not living in that death trap masquerading as a house.

When they finally had the fire under control, he helped stow the gear, his gaze searching for Lindsey and Josh. He figured the police had gotten the Red Cross involved to help relocate the family that had just lost their home. There was no way he was going to allow Lindsey and Josh to return to their place either, not until he'd had the structure thoroughly checked out.

Might be a good idea to check the electrical wiring in the house, too. He had a sneaking suspicion it wasn't up to code, as the footprint of Lindsey's house was exactly the same as the one that had gone up in flames. Just the thought of faulty wiring lining the walls made his blood run cold.

"Lindsey?" He made his way over to where she and Josh both stood, looking a bit shocked, their arms wrapped around each other for support. "I'll take you over to my place for what's left of the night, OK?"

She frowned. "We can't go back to our house?"

"Not yet. There could be a fair amount of water and smoke damage." He was glad he didn't have to lie—there had been a lot of water damage in particular. "I'm afraid the house needs to be cleared by us before you can move back in."

"Oh." She bit her lip and shrugged. "Well, then, a hotel is fine. We don't need to impose on you."

Stubborn woman. He ground his teeth in frustration. "You're not imposing." Just once he wished she'd simply give in and let him help. Although she didn't realize how much his need to help was wrapped up in his guilt over being the cause of Sam's death. "Actually, it might be better if you drove your car so you're not stranded without a set of wheels."

She seemed to like that idea, but still hesitated. "I don't know—a hotel might be better if this is going to take a while."

"A few days at the most," Austin told her, even though he didn't point out that if the house needed repairs, the timeframe would undoubtedly be longer. "Please? At least for tonight?"

She grudgingly nodded. "Can we pack some of our things?"

"Sure." He was grateful to give her at least that much. His crew was standing around, waiting for him, but he waved the guys off, figuring he'd get a ride back to the fire station with Lindsey, and followed her inside.

The place was even smaller than he'd realized. Frowning at the open, rumpled sofa sleeper taking up most of the living room, he watched as she gathered some clothes together, throwing them into an old, well-worn suitcase.

He didn't like the circumstances she was living in, that's for sure. For Pete's sake, she didn't even have a bedroom of her own. Once again he wondered what had happened? What had caused her to move from the nice three-bedroom house she'd lived in with Sam to this?

What's more, knowing she'd moved without telling him hurt.

Had she deliberately moved just to avoid him?

Lindsey closed the suitcase and bent over to pick it up.

"I'll take that," he said, stepping forward to lift the heavy case from her grasp. He lugged the case outside and put it in the trunk of Lindsey's bright yellow Plymouth Neon. Lindsey loved yellow cars and the bright yellow color usually made him smile, but not tonight. After returning inside, he went back to find Lindsey and Josh in the single bedroom located at the rear of the house. Josh's suitcase was full, as well, so Austin took it before Lindsey could.

"Anything else?" he asked, when he'd stored Josh's suitcase in the trunk, too.

"I guess not." Lindsey gave one last glance around the compact kitchen and living room area with a forlorn gaze.

"Hey, don't worry, you'll be back soon," he murmured, placing a hand in the small of her back and gently urging her toward the door. "Come on, let's go. You guys need some sleep. I have a spare bedroom at my place you can use. Two of them, actually." She'd only been to his place once so she might not know how many bedrooms he had. She and Josh would be far better off in his place than staying in the tiny house, even if the place was safe to move back into. At least this way they'd each have their own bedroom.

"Thank heavens tomorrow is Sunday," Lindsey said, with a wide yawn. "Josh will be able to rest before he has to head back to school."

"Do you have to work tomorrow?" he asked. Lindsey was an ED nurse for the Sun Valley Community Hospital and he'd always enjoyed seeing her when he'd brought patients in from his paramedic runs.

"No." She shook her head. "Not until Monday."

Good. He was glad she'd have a day to recuperate, as well. He was tempted to take over the task of driving, but knew Lindsey would be irritated if he tried to take control, so he forced himself to hand Lindsey her car keys. She raised a brow, a smile tugging at the corner of her mouth, as if she knew what the small gesture had cost him. With a sigh he took off his bulky jacket and hat so he could slide into the passenger seat.

"You can stay with me for as long as you need to," he said in a low tone as she drove to his house, located not far from the home she'd shared with Sam, his partner and his best friend.

"Thanks, but one night should be enough." She barely glanced at him, her attention on the road. He didn't contradict her, hoping he could convince her to stay if her house needed repairs. At least for a while.

She fell silent, so he contented himself with watching her. She was beautiful, even with her long blonde hair mussed and not a speck of makeup on her face. He had a hard time tearing his gaze from her profile.

Knock it off, Monroe, he warned himself. Stop thinking of Lindsey as a woman you're attracted to. He'd promised Sam he'd take care of them.

Lindsey needed a friend right now. A helping hand. A shoulder to lean on.

Not a man who fantasized about being more.

A fresh wave of guilt hit low in his belly. First he'd cost his partner his life, robbing Lindsey and Josh of a husband and father. Then he'd botched his attempts to help her. What was wrong with him that he lusted after his best friend's widow?

Could he sink any lower?

Women had come and gone in the course of his life, but it hadn't been something he'd worried about. He'd never had to work very hard to attract a pretty woman's attention. Settling down with just one female partner had never appealed to him. Although he came from a large family with lots of brothers and sisters, and parents who'd been married for over forty years, he'd figured he wasn't the type to settle down.

So why was he so interested in the one woman who had marriage and family written all over her? A woman with a nine-year-old son who needed a father?

A woman he'd promised his best friend he'd take care of?

He gave himself a mental shake. He'd always admired Lindsey from afar, but she was strictly off-limits. The sooner his hormones figured that out, the better off he'd be.

CHAPTER TWO

WHEN Lindsey woke up, the window was on the wrong side of the room. She blinked, disoriented by her strange surroundings, and then gradually realized where she was.

Austin's house. She and Josh were sleeping in the two spare bedrooms of Austin's house after their neighbor's horrible house fire. Thank heavens no one had been hurt.

The tantalizing aroma of bacon and eggs made her stomach growl, reminding her it had been way too many hours since her last meal.

If you could even call macaroni and cheese out of a box a meal.

Scrambling from the wide bed, she headed for the shower. When she emerged, feeling much more awake and refreshed, she noticed the door of Josh's room was ajar and her son was nowhere in sight.

He was probably already downstairs, helping himself to Austin's breakfast. Good thing her son had always gotten along with Austin. The poor kid had been through enough trauma lately, between his problems at school and the recent move away from his friends.

She hastily dressed and then took a few minutes to blow-dry her hair. Not because she was vain and wanted to look nice for Austin, she told herself as she headed down to the kitchen, but because she wanted to be ready so she could do whatever needed to be done to obtain permission to move back into her house.

If she had her way, they wouldn't be imposing on Austin's hospitality for long.

"Hi," Austin greeted her, his gaze warm and appreciative as it swept over her. Her mouth went dry as she stared at him. Austin stood in front of the stove, wearing a tight, paramedic blue T-shirt that emphasized his broad shoulders and a pair of well-worn jeans that rode low on his hips. His mahogany-colored hair was long and a bit shaggy. Holding a spatula in his hand didn't come close to compromising his masculinity.

Liar. Who was she trying to kid? This was the real reason she'd taken time with her appearance. Heavens, what was wrong with her? Why couldn't she control this ridiculous attraction to Austin? Taking a deep breath, she glanced to where Josh was seated at the table, his mouth full of crunchy bacon. "Good morning." She kept her tone light. "Austin, you didn't have to cook for us. I'm sure we could have gotten by with cereal this morning."

He gave a negligent shrug, dividing his attention between her and the eggs in the frying pan. "I cooked for myself, but made enough for everyone. If you're hungry, have a seat."

She was famished, so she pulled up a chair across from Josh and sat down. As if on cue, Austin set a plate in front of her with two eggs cooked over easy, wheat toast and two slices of bacon.

Everything made exactly the way she liked it.

His thoughtfulness made her throat close and for a moment she couldn't speak. This was why she'd avoided Austin in the months since Sam's death. Being this close to him was painful because every moment with him only magnified Sam's shortcomings as a husband. He and Sam may have been friends, but they couldn't have been more different.

"Thanks," she murmured, avoiding his gaze and turning her attention to her food. When he took a seat beside her, she was all too aware of his presence.

The cozy atmosphere in the kitchen was almost too much to bear. She couldn't remember the last time Sam had joined her and Josh for a family meal. For too long Sam had insisted in sitting in front of the television to eat, claiming he needed to relax after his long days at work. They'd grown so far apart over the years since Josh's birth, sometimes she'd looked at him and wondered how she'd fallen out of love with him so quickly.

Or if she'd ever really loved Sam the way he deserved to be loved at all?

She slammed a door on the excruciating memories.

"Do you have to go back to the fire station?" she asked, glancing at Austin. She knew from Sam's schedule, the firefighter-paramedic crew were usually scheduled for twenty-four hours on duty, then off for forty-eight, unless they were needed for additional shifts.

"No, I'm off duty as of this morning."

"Did you get much sleep?" She'd taken him back to the fire station last night after he'd brought their suitcases in and had gotten them settled. It had been late before she'd tumbled into bed, close to two in the morning. He must have gotten even less sleep than she had.

"Enough." He shrugged again, and his smile was crooked. "I'm used to interrupted sleep with my schedule. It's hard to sleep after the adrenaline rush of fighting fires. Although I have to admit, it was harder to sleep knowing you'd moved into a house on Puckett Street without telling me."

She focused her attention on her food, wishing she could think of a way to avoid this conversation. "I did mail you a change-of-address note and there's nothing wrong with living on Puckett Street."

"Yes, there is. None of my friends live there," Josh argued.

Lindsey stifled a sigh. She and Josh had been over this too many times to count. "I'm sure you'll make new friends. And I've been driving you over to your friend's house when I can."

Austin frowned. "I didn't get a note."

He hadn't? She frowned, knowing she'd sent it. "Must have gotten lost in the mail." She tried to change the subject. "Do you know what caused the Tollivers' fire?"

"Faulty wiring." He finished his food in record time, the same way Sam always had. Must be part of the firefighter's strategy—to eat quick before the next call. "Your house has the same footprint and likely built by the same company, so I'd really like to have a professional check out the wiring before you move back in. Especially now, with the potential water damage, too. We drenched your house pretty good to prevent the fire from spreading."

Her heart sank. What he said made sense, but she didn't want to be dependent on him. Hadn't she become too dependent on him the last time he'd tried to help? Staying with Austin was dangerous to her emotional well-being. Being independent was important to her, now more than ever. "Maybe someone can come out first thing Monday morning?"

Austin slowly nodded. "I'll see what I can do."

It was on the tip of her tongue to suggest she could make her own arrangements, but then realized she wouldn't really know where to start. How many electricians did she know? None. Obviously, she'd be stupid to refuse Austin's expertise.

At least for this. But if he tried to take over

other aspects of her life, she'd have no choice but to leave.

"Can I be excused?" Josh asked, pushing away from the table. "Tony and I want to go skateboarding."

Austin opened his mouth as if to respond, but then closed it again when she raised a brow at him. She turned to her son. "Sure. Be back home by dinnertime, though."

"Thanks, Mom." Josh disappeared from the kitchen.

"Thanks for not interfering," she said to Austin, admiring his restraint.

"You're welcome." He hesitated, and then added, "Lindsey, I know the last time we saw each other, you were very angry with me. I'm sorry if you felt I tried to take over your life. I never meant to hurt you in any way. I care about you and Josh—you're Sam's family, for heaven's sake. You must know I only want to help. Please, make yourself at home here, OK?"

He was being too nice. Again. She tried not to

feel guilty as he threw her words back at her. She had basically told him to stop interfering in her life and to leave her alone. During thosc first few weeks, right after Sam's death, Austin had been glued to her side. She'd appreciated his strength and his compassion, but after a while, when he'd continued to make decisions for her, especially about Josh, she'd gotten annoyed. The fact that he was so darn attractive didn't help matters either.

If she was honest, she'd admit that she'd pushed Austin away as much because she was attracted to him as because he had been trying to take over her life. Both were equally dangerous. She needed to remain strong enough to resist him. "Austin, I know you're only trying to help but, please, understand how important it is to me that I'm able to stand on my own two feet."

"Is that why you sold Sam's house?" he asked.

"No." She stood, and began clearing the breakfast dishes from the table. "As you cooked, it's only fair I clean up."

He caught her arm. "Lindsey, did you sell the house because you couldn't afford it?"

"What difference does it make?" She subtly tried to tug her arm from his grasp.

"It makes a lot of difference. I could have given you the money to make your house payments until you received the company life insurance payment."

"I don't want your money, Austin." She jerked out of his grasp. What part of being independent didn't he understand? She wasn't like her mother. She didn't need a man in order to survive. She could manage just fine by herself. "My financial situation isn't any of your concern."

Austin tried to stay out of Lindsey's way for the remainder of the day. It wasn't easy. His three-bedroom house didn't seem nearly as spacious with Lindsey and Josh there.

Not that he was complaining. He was grateful she'd allowed him to help this much. He didn't understand why she was so dead set against leaning on him. It didn't take a rocket scientist to figure out Sam must have left some debts. As Sam had died on the job, Lindsey should have gotten a payment from the company's life insurance policy.

Enough of a payment that she wouldn't have needed to sell the house and move.

He scowled, wishing he'd known about her financial difficulties. He never should have listened to her and backed off. But then again he'd never imagined she'd be forced to move either. All this time he'd been imaging her and Josh living in their nice house, getting back into the normal routine. In fact, he'd seen her a few times over the past two months since he'd been at work in California, but had simply said hi and asked how things were, without getting into anything personal.

Concern nagged at him as he made phone calls, leaving messages with several contractors about Lindsey's house. If he had his way, he'd put the stupid thing on the market. She and Josh could live with him until they got back on their feet.

He winced inwardly. Yeah. Like she'd allow that to happen. Not. Give it up, Monroe.

"Do you have any laundry that needs to be done?" Lindsey asked, standing in the doorway of the living room. "Our clothes smell like smoke."

"Ah, sure." *Do not imagine Lindsey touching your boxers,* he told himself as he fetched the laundry from the hamper in the bathroom. "Are you sure you don't mind?"

"Why should I?" she asked with a careless shrug. "May as well combine loads."

She acted like doing his laundry was no big deal, but in all the years since he'd left home no woman had ever done his laundry. Sharing these sorts of chores seemed more intimate than it should. And the awkward mood surrounding them was driving him crazy. He wished she'd relax, but it seemed as though Lindsey was constantly in motion, doing one thing or another.

When Josh returned from skateboarding,

Austin suggested they all go out to grab something to eat. At first Lindsey looked like she wanted to argue, but then she agreed.

He took them to a nearby family restaurant, unsure of what foods, other than pizza, Josh liked to eat. Apparently he'd chosen well when Josh grew excited over the variety of menu options.

"The new subdivision across the street from our old house is awesome for skateboarding," Josh said, once the waitress had taken their order. "You should see the houses, Mom, they're really cool."

Lindsey simply raised a brow. "I'm glad you and Tony had fun. What else did you do besides skateboarding?"

"We hung out at his house—he has the newest video and it's so sweet…" His voice trailed off and suddenly he slouched down in his seat, picking up his plastic cup of soda and holding it in front of his face.

Austin glanced around to see what had caused Josh's sudden change from chatterbox to mute.

He caught sight of a police officer in full uniform sliding into a booth not far from theirs with his son, who looked to be about Josh's age. He frowned. A friend from school? If so, Josh didn't look so happy to see him.

"Sit up," Lindsey said with an annoyed frown. "Don't spill."

Josh sat up a fraction of an inch, and continued to blow bubbles into his glass with his straw. Austin could tell he was hoping the other kid didn't see him.

"So what's your favorite subject in school?" Austin asked, trying to change the subject. He edged his chair over, hopefully obstructing the kid's view of Josh from the booth.

"I dunno." Josh shrugged, still slouching in his seat.

"Come on, you must have a favorite," Austin urged. "English? Math? History? Science?"

"Math is OK, I guess."

Lindsey glanced at him in surprise. "Just OK? What are you talking about? You love math."

Josh didn't answer as the waitress chose that moment to bring their food.

As they ate, Josh didn't say more than two words unless asked. Austin wondered what the heck was up with Josh and the cop's son, but he decided he'd wait until he and Josh were alone to ask.

Lindsey didn't seem to notice Josh's silence. Would she resent his interference if he did ask Josh what was going on? Or would she remind him Josh wasn't his concern? He didn't want her to tell him again to leave her alone.

Especially as Lindsey and Josh shouldn't be alone. Sam should have been here with them.

Sam's death had been his fault. Over these last few months the truth had been gnawing at him. Maybe it was time he confessed to Lindsey how he had been the cause of Sam's death.

"Lindsey, your next admission has been placed in room six."

"Thanks." Lindsey flashed a quick smile at the ED charge nurse and glanced at the clock hanging over the main board, amazed to realize her shift was nearly over. These short, six-hour fill-in shifts were wonderful, especially while Josh was in school.

But then her smile faded as the reality of her situation set in. Short shifts were nice, but she really needed to try to pick up more hours to pay for home owner's insurance. Yet with all the trouble Josh had gotten into over these past few months, the thought of leaving him home alone, even for an hour, bothered her. She'd prided herself on always being home for him.

Shaking off her troublesome thoughts, she read the name listed beside bed number six on the main ED board where the patient's names automatically lit up the moment they were registered in Triage. Her next patient was Blaine Larson, a sixteen-year-old with a possible concussion he'd sustained during a fistfight.

"Great," Lindsey murmured under her breath. "I hope this isn't where Josh is headed." Skipping school and arguments in the playground were bad enough—she couldn't take it if Josh started fighting.

With a sigh she picked up the clipboard set up for bed six and glanced down at the initial information the triage nurse had collected. Blaine was awake and alert but was only oriented to his name and place. He was confused about the date and time. Otherwise, his vital signs were stable.

She grabbed her stethoscope and headed into the room. Blaine was a tall, broad-shouldered, nice-looking, clean-cut kid. He had a large welt on his lip, but no other obvious outward signs of trauma. With closed head injuries, though, the worst part of the damage was hidden from the naked eye.

"Hi, Blaine, my name is Lindsey. I'll be your nurse. Tell me what happened."

"I don't remember. But from what I've been told, me and some of my friends were arguing with these jock football players and one of them slugged me in the face."

"Hmm." She glanced over at Blaine's mother

seated next to his cart, then looked back at the patient. "Can you answer a few questions for me? What's your full name?"

"Blaine Michael Larson."

"What day is it?"

"I don't know." He glanced over to his mother for help. Lindsey subtly shook her head, indicating his mother shouldn't answer.

"Do you know the month?" Lindsey persisted.

"Uh, July? No, wait. It has to be August."

Not even close. She frowned. "What about the year? Do you know what year it is?"

"No." Blaine shook his head. "All I know is that someone hit me in the face."

"Where are you? What is this place?" Lindsey asked.

"A hospital. Sun Valley Community Hospital."

"That's right." Lindsey smiled, taking a penlight out of her pocket and flashing it in the boy's eyes. His pupils looked equal and reactive to light. They weren't overly dilated or misshapen. "Does your head hurt?"

"No." Blaine frowned and gently fingered his bruised lip. "But my mouth hurts."

"I'm sure it does." Lindsey glanced at Blaine's mother. "Do you know if he lost consciousness?"

"Yes, apparently for a few seconds he did." Blaine's mother sighed. "I don't know why he was in a fight. He normally gets along fine with people."

Lindsey nodded, thinking the same thing about Josh. In the past he'd got along fine with the other kids at school, too. Only lately he'd been complaining of stomachaches in the morning. And his grades were slipping, no doubt a result of his skipping school. With everything that had happened after losing Sam, her son had turned into a complete stranger.

And she didn't know how to get him back.

"OK, I'm going to listen to his heart and lungs, and then we'll have the doctor come and take a look. I think we'll probably get a CT scan of his head, just to make sure everything's all right."

"I understand," Mrs Larson said.

Lindsey did a quick assessment but other than his lack of memory Blaine appeared to be a healthy sixteen-year-old. After writing up her findings, she went out to report to the ED physician.

The physician on duty was Dr Markham. He examined Blaine Larson and then ordered blood work and a CT scan of his head.

"What about a drug screen?" Lindsey asked. "I mean, I know he's sixteen, but shouldn't we check, just in case?"

"Not a bad idea. Let me ask his mother." Dr Markham took Blaine's mother aside, and after a brief conversation with her he came back. "Yes, add a urine drug and alcohol screen. She said she's never caught him doing any drugs or drinking, but it's best to make sure."

"OK." Lindsey called the radiology department to arrange the CT scan then quickly went in to draw Blaine's blood. To be on the safe side, she placed a twenty-gauge capped IV in his antecubital vein. "You're going to feel a poke here," she warned.

"Ouch," Blaine yelped when she slid the needle in.

"All done." She drew the blood off and then taped down the catheter and capped off the line in case they needed it later. "Someone will be here shortly to take you to Radiology. We're going to get a scan of your head to make sure there's no bleeding in there."

"All right." Blaine was pretty cooperative, considering the gaps in his memory. Some head-injury patients could get very aggressive.

Lindsey checked on her other patients, one was an elderly man who was waiting to be admitted to a hospital bed for management of his congestive heart failure and the other patient a young girl who'd broken her wrist falling out of a tree. All in all, a quiet day as far as shifts in the ED went.

She took five minutes to eat a sandwich she'd brought from Austin's house while Blaine was getting his CT scan. She hoped she and Josh would be able to move back home soon. It was sweet of

Austin to lend them a hand, but sharing his house with him was much harder than she'd imagined.

Even worse was the deeper temptation to let Austin solve her problems. She knew he would if she so much as dropped a hint.

No. She needed to be strong. Jumping up when she saw Blaine being wheeled back, she went over to meet him, glad to hear the results were negative. She checked on his laboratory work before going to talk to Dr Markham again.

"Everything on Blaine Larson is negative." She handed him the lab results which she'd printed off the computer. "Including his drug screen."

"Hmm. Good, I guess he's OK to be discharged, then, but his mother needs to keep an eye on him for the next twenty-four hours."

"I'll give her the informational brochures on how to take care of a concussion." Lindsey had already pulled the information off the computer and lifted the sheets of paper from the printer tray. They had a ready reference for common ailments online.

She'd just finished giving Blaine's mother the instructions, making sure she understood what to watch for in case Blaine's confusion grew worse, when she heard her name being called.

"Lindsey? You have a call on line two from Sun Valley Elementary School."

The school? Josh. She hurried over to pick up the phone. "Hello, this is Lindsey Winters."

"Mrs Winters? This is Eric Dolan, Principal of Sun Valley School. We have Josh here in our office. He's been caught skipping school again. You'll need to come in."

No, not again. She closed her eyes and rubbed her temple. Dear heaven, what was wrong with him? This was the second time this month. Then barely a week before that she'd been called because he'd used foul language on the playground. Her sweet son, using bad language. She could hardly believe it. "I'm at work, but I'll do my best to leave."

"We'll be waiting." Principal Dolan didn't sound too sympathetic.

With a sick feeling in her stomach, Lindsey hung up the phone and found the charge nurse. "I'm sorry, but I need to go. Josh is in trouble. Again."

Sue glanced at the clock. "Well, your shift is over in thirty minutes anyway, so that's fine. We'll cover your patients."

"Thanks." Lindsey gave report on the status of her remaining patients then left. Outside, in her car, she hesitated, thinking about Austin. As much as she wanted to be independent, there was no denying Josh needed someone to talk to. She'd noticed how Austin had tried to draw Josh out over dinner last night, trying to break her son's bad mood.

For a moment she rested her head on the steering wheel. Austin was the last guy she should lean on for strength. He was far too appealing. Too nice. Too attractive.

Too single!

He was just being nice with his repeated offers to help. And she understood. He tried to help because he was Sam's friend and wanted to look after her. He had a reputation throughout the ED of being a womanizer, going from one nurse to another. She refused to stand in line.

Besides, he certainly hadn't asked for her to be attracted to him. He thought she was the grieving widow. He had no idea how strained things had gotten between her and Sam before his death.

In fact, she was convinced Sam's death was her fault. He had probably been upset and not thinking clearly during the wildfire because she'd filed for divorce right before he'd left on his last smoke jumping mission.

CHAPTER THREE

AUSTIN was standing in Lindsey's house, assessing the water damage in the corner of her living room, when his phone rang. He recognized Lindsey's number. "Hello?"

"Austin. I'm sorry to bother you, but I need your help." Her voice sounded thick, as if she was near tears. "I just got a call from the school. Josh's in trouble. Again."

He frowned, thinking Josh had seemed perfectly fine yesterday. Well, except for his withdrawal at dinner. "What happened?"

"He was picked up by the police for skipping school again," she admitted.

"He skipped school?" Again? Why hadn't she said anything about the first time?

"Yes." She sniffled loudly. "It started a couple of months ago, right before we moved. He's been skipping school and once I was called because he used bad language on the playground. I just don't know what has gotten into him. He won't talk to me, but I thought you might have better luck. Will you come?"

He didn't hesitate. "I'll be right there."

"Good. Thanks."

"No problem. I'll meet you at the school." Austin closed his cell phone and then glanced at the contractor he'd hired to go over Lindsey's house. "I want a full report within the hour on what needs to be completed to bring this place up to code."

"Will do," the contractor agreed.

Satisfied, he left Lindsey's house and jumped into his truck. The elementary school in Sun Valley wasn't too far, although the house Lindsey had shared with Sam had been much closer. Pushing the speed limit as much as he dared, he made it to the school in fifteen minutes. He parked next to Lindsey's bright yellow car and walked into the building, looking for the principal's office.

Instinctively, he knew where it was. He'd spent a few hours in the principal's office when he'd been a kid, too.

He found Lindsey was already there, wearing her green hospital scrubs, her arm looped around Josh's thin young shoulders. The kid was staring at the floor, as if he wished he could just disappear.

"Mrs Winters, surely you understand that this behavior of Josh's has to stop. This is the fourth incident over the past two months. His grades have deteorated, and if you don't figure out a way to keep him from skipping school, I'm afraid he may need to repeat the fourth grade."

"I understand." Lindsey's desperate gaze caught Austin's. His stomach squeezed in sympathy. First Sam's death, then moving to a new house, then the fire and now this. He had a feeling she couldn't take much more.

"Have you taken our advice and arranged

counseling for Josh?" the principal asked in a perplexed tone.

Austin was surprised when she nodded. "Yes." Lindsey glanced down at Josh, who stared stubbornly at the toes of his shoes. "Dr Ellen Sandberg is convinced that Josh's anger and lack of interest in school is directly related to the loss of his father."

Austin hadn't known Josh was seeing a psychologist. What else didn't he know?

"Hmm." The principal's expression was serious. "That may be, Mrs Winters, and, of course, we're very sorry about your loss. I'm sure this is a difficult time for both of you. But Josh is certainly old enough to understand right from wrong, and skipping out of school is wrong." The principal spread his hands in a helpless gesture. "I'm not sure what you expect us to do. We can't pass him if he doesn't go to school."

"I know." Austin saw Lindsey's grip tighten on Josh's shoulder. "Josh won't do it again."

When Josh hunched his shoulders and stubbed

his toe into the floor, Austin wasn't so sure about that.

"Josh?" he stepped forward, joining the conversation. "What happened? Why did you skip school?"

Josh shrugged and glanced up at Austin, defiance reflected in his blue eyes. "I dunno."

"'I don't know' is not an acceptable answer," Lindsey said in a sharp tone. "How do you expect to pass if you don't go to school?"

He understood Lindsey's frustration, but there had to be more going on here. Did Josh miss Sam that much? His gut clenched. He hadn't lost his father, so he couldn't even begin to imagine how Josh was coping. Was he lonely? Josh seemed to have at least one friend, Tony. Austin had grown up in a rowdy, noisy family with lots of brothers and sisters. He'd never been lonely, even when he'd wanted to be left alone.

"He needs to serve a detention. And make up the work he's missed," the principal continued.

"You'll have to talk to his teacher to arrange for the completion of all his missing assignments."

Austin could see all this talk about extra homework was only making Josh feel worse. Not that he shouldn't do the work, but there was no sense dwelling on it.

"Let's go," he said in a low tone to Lindsey.

She nodded, understanding his desire to talk to Josh outside the school. "I'll be in touch with Josh's teacher," Lindsey said.

The principal stood. "Mrs Winters, I'd like to receive a report from his counselor prior to allowing him back into class. I need to know there isn't something more going on here with Josh's truancy."

"I understand." Lindsey's worried frown brought a wave of helpless anger over Austin. She shouldn't have to bear the burden of all this alone. She tugged Josh's arm. "Come on, let's go."

Josh followed her out, looking completely dejected. Austin felt bad for the kid. What in the world had happened? There had to be a reason he was acting like he was. Because of the move? It didn't seem like a mere move would be enough to cause him to skip school. Josh had always been a nice kid, had never been in trouble before that he was aware of.

"I'm sorry to bother you," Lindsey said, as they walked through the parking lot to their respective cars. They'd managed to stay out of each other's way that morning as she'd got Josh up and ready for school and then left for work.

"It's not a big deal. In fact, I was out at your house, talking to the contractor." He glanced at Josh, who lagged behind as if he didn't want to be near either of the adults. "We'll meet at my house, OK? I'd like to try talking to Josh alone, man-to-man."

Lindsey nodded and he figured it was a sign of how upset she was that she didn't jump on his comment about the contractor. "Do you think he'll talk to you, Austin? So far, Dr Sandberg hasn't had much luck."

"I don't know, but I'd like to try." Austin

opened the driver's side car door for her. When she leaned close to get in, her subtle clean scent teased his senses. His body reacted, as it always did around Lindsey. Most of the time he thought he hid his physical response pretty well. And when he felt himself losing the battle, distance worked to put things back into perspective.

Although he'd discovered distance was much harder to achieve when they were living together under the same roof.

She hesitated, putting her hand over his on the top of the car door. His pulse leapt at the light touch. "I'd appreciate it if you would talk to him, Austin. I just don't understand what has gotten into him over these past few months."

For a moment he stared at their hands, wishing he could pull her close, but then she turned away, sliding into the car. Josh had climbed into the passenger seat and was staring sullenly out the window. Austin took a deep breath, forcing himself to maintain control.

"I'll see you at…my place." He'd almost said

"home." As if Lindsey and Josh belonged there with him. Giving himself a mental shake, he closed the car door and waited until she pulled out before climbing into his truck to follow.

The ride to his house was short. He pulled into his driveway, parking beside Lindsey's car. He strode inside, finding Lindsey and Josh seated in the living room. Josh looked miserable and, sitting next to him, Lindsey didn't look much better. He hated the deep grooves of worry around her eyes.

She rose to her feet when she saw him. "I'll let you guys talk while I throw in some laundry." She caught herself, and looked at him askance. "If you don't mind?"

"Of course not," he hastened to reassure her. Damn, he didn't want her to feel like a guest, he wanted her to be comfortable. "I told you to make yourself at home."

She nodded and disappeared into the kitchen. He didn't think she'd appreciate knowing how much he liked having her there to share the housekeeping chores. Actually, he wouldn't even have minded doing most of the work himself, as long as she stayed with him. Tearing his mind from these ridiculous thoughts, he turned to look at Josh and gestured to the vacant spot on the sofa. "Do you mind if I sit down?"

Josh shrugged, but didn't make eye contact. Austin purposely sat next to him, trying to think of a way to get the boy to open up to him. "Josh, I think I know what you're going through."

Josh glanced at him in surprise. "You do?"

Austin nodded. "I know you miss your dad very much. I guess school doesn't seem very important right now, does it?"

Josh slowly shook his head. "No."

"Are the kids teasing you? Or are you just sad over missing your dad?"

Josh was quiet for so long he figured the boy wouldn't answer. When he finally spoke, Austin had to lean forward in order to hear him. "The first time I skipped school, Bobby's dad caught me. Bobby's been making fun of me ever since."

A cop's son? The kid in the restaurant last

night. Josh's strange behavior was starting to make sense. He and Bobby, the cop's son, obviously had a history.

"He has no right to make fun of you, Josh, but continuing to skip school isn't going to help. Did Bobby's dad find you again today?"

Josh nodded, his face grim.

Figured. The kid just couldn't catch a break. "Look, Josh, I know school seems stupid right now, but you have to pull yourself together. The last thing you need right now is to fail your classes. Do you think your dad would want you to skip school?"

"No." Josh hunched his shoulders again. "But sometimes I'm so sad I can't stand it. I leave, because I don't want anyone else to see me cry."

Oh, man. He could completely understand. He wrapped his arm around Josh's thin shoulders. "Josh, I also cried when your dad died. It's nothing to be ashamed of."

Josh swiped his face against his arm and sniffled loudly. "I just miss him."

"I know you do." He held onto Josh tight, wishing more than anything he'd been the one to die that day instead of Sam. "I miss him, too."

For a long moment they hung onto each other, sharing their grief. He glanced over to see Lindsey working in the kitchen, keeping busy. These past few months must have been just as hard on her.

"Why didn't you tell your mom about this, Josh?" he asked, when Josh finally pushed away.

"I didn't want her to feel sad, too. She always looks like she's going to cry when I talk about my dad."

Protecting his mom. Austin couldn't say anything—he probably would have done the same thing.

"I wish I didn't have to see Bobby at school tomorrow," Josh muttered.

"Somehow, you have to learn to ignore Bobby," Austin said firmly. "He's just a kid. There must be some way you can avoid him."

Josh shrugged. "I've tried to stay away, but he always finds me."

"Is that when you were caught using bad language on the playground?" Austin surmised.

"Yeah."

Bobby was starting to sound a bit like a bully. Josh needed something else to do, something to help take his mind off missing his dad. "OK, here's what we're going to do. We're going to find something for you to do. Do you like sports?"

"Sort of," Josh said without enthusiasm.

Austin racked his brains, trying to think. Bobby was probably into sports, so Josh needed something different. He remembered the Tai Kwon Do studio he had passed on the way to the elementary school. "What about learning martial arts?"

Josh perked up. "That might be cool."

Good. So far, so good. "OK, I'll talk to your mom about this. But Josh, you really need to stay in school. Just avoid Bobby and his friends. Your grades have to be top priority."

"Can Tony learn Tai Kwon Do with me?" Josh asked.

"Sure. If your grades don't suffer." He suspected this idea wasn't going to go over really well with Lindsey, especially considering her financial difficulties, but he'd do his best to convince her. Josh needed something to focus on, something that would help him deal with missing his dad. The martial arts were all about being spiritually strong, as well as physically strong. He thought maybe it could work. "I'll talk to your mom and see if we can work out you guys taking classes together."

"Cool." For the first time since seeing Josh sitting in the principal's office, he saw a spark of interest flare in the boy's eyes.

"Just remember, your grades have to improve," Austin warned. "Homework has to come first."

"I know." Josh nodded. "I can pull up my grades, they're not that bad." When Austin raised a disbelieving brow, Josh's chin dropped to his chest and he added, "Well, maybe they are bad, but I'll make up all my missing assignments."

"I'm glad." He wanted to believe Josh would pull himself together. "And I'm here if you ever want to talk about your dad."

"OK."

Austin stood, glancing toward the kitchen to where Lindsey was busy with the laundry. She looked so beautiful, with her blonde hair falling in waves to her shoulders, he had to physically steel himself against the need to pull her close. "Why don't you get started on those missing assignments right now, while I talk to your mom?"

Josh frowned. "Are you going to tell her why I've been skipping school?"

Austin hesitated, not wanting to break the boy's trust. Yet at the same time he didn't want to lie to Lindsey either. "Josh, I'm sure your mom understands how much you miss your dad."

"But I don't want her to be sad, too," Josh protested.

Austin understood. Josh didn't want to contribute to her grief. "I know, but she loves you and needs to know you're OK. Telling her might help her agree to send you to Tai Kwon Do classes."

Josh grimaced but then nodded. "All right," he agreed grudgingly.

Austin turned toward the kitchen, wishing he felt as confident as he sounded. Unease tightened his gut.

He and Lindsey needed to talk, about more than just the repairs on her house. Josh needed someone to talk to, someone he could relate to. He wanted to be there, for both of them.

He needed to fulfill his promise to Sam.

Somehow he needed to convince her to let him help this time.

Lindsey was grateful Dr Ellen Sandberg had returned her phone call so quickly. She nodded at Austin when he came into the kitchen and continued her conversation. "I need to make an appointment for Josh, as soon as possible. He skipped school again and they won't let him back into class until you see him."

"All right. I could probably squeeze him in later this afternoon, say about five o'clock?" Dr Sandberg offered.

"Five would be great. Thanks so much." Relieved, she hung up the phone. Austin's presence in the kitchen made it seem smaller than normal.

She was conscious of how Austin intently watched her as she folded a load of clothes. She flushed under his scrutiny and hoped he'd blame her red cheeks on the heat from the dryer.

"Do you think I could go with him?" Austin asked.

"With who?" Flustered, she glanced at him. "You mean with Josh? To his psychologist's appointment?"

"Yeah." Austin tucked his hands into the front pockets of his jeans. "I'd like to go with him tonight to see Dr Sandberg. The appointment is at five, right?"

Surprised, she stopped folding clothes to stare at him. She couldn't believe he was actually offering to go with Josh. When things had started going downhill between her and Sam, she'd suggested marriage counseling, but Sam had flatly refused to attend. He hadn't believed there had been anything counseling could do to change things.

"I…uh…don't see why not. Although we'd have to get Dr. Sandberg's approval." She hastily glanced away, wishing Austin wasn't so appealing. He looked so good, even wearing nothing more than a casual T-shirt and well-worn denim jeans. He smelt great, too. For a moment she remembered how he'd stood at her side throughout Sam's funeral. It had taken every ounce of willpower she'd possessed not to lean on his rugged strength. To keep him at a safe distance.

She wasn't some pathetic widow who needed a man to get by. Sam hadn't deserved to die, but she'd already planned to live her life without him. Jumping into a relationship with another man wasn't part of her plan. No matter how difficult things were, she wasn't going to be like her mother, leaping headfirst into a new relationship the moment the previous one ended. Lindsey had suffered through three stepfathers, not to mention some boyfriends in between. None of the guys her mother had hooked up with had been a contender for father of the year.

"Here, let me help." He crossed over and pitched in, picking up a shirt and folding it. She subtly stepped away, trying to give him more room. The muscles of his arms rippled with the simple movement and she remembered the day Austin had come out to help Sam fix the leaky place in the roof. He'd stripped off his shirt, displaying the bronze muscles of his shoulders and chest to full advantage.

Not that Sam had been a wimp, but for all Austin's strength there was a gentleness, as well, a softness or a caring that her husband had seemed to lose somewhere along the ten-year course of their marriage.

Stop remembering the worst, she told herself sternly. Sam wasn't a bad guy, there just had been something...missing. Sam was gone, there was no reason to dwell on what had failed in their marriage.

Austin looked good, whether he was doing housework or repairing the roof. She had to stop comparing him to Sam. She needed to focus on Josh, not her inappropriate reaction to her husband's best friend.

Besides, even if she had been in the market for a man, Austin wasn't her type. She knew from Sam that Austin didn't lack female company. Sam had gone on and on about how single women flocked to his friend. He'd claimed Austin never dated the same woman twice. She'd often suspected Sam had been jealous because Austin had been single and Sam hadn't.

Thank heavens she wasn't looking for a relationship, or she might have become obsessed with Austin, too.

Annoyed with herself, she finished folding the laundry and stepped back. "We should probably consider an easy dinner, as Josh has his appointment at five."

"Lindsey—" he began, but then halted when his phone rang. "Hello? Hi, Mark. Tell me what you found."

She listened, belatedly realizing Austin had to be talking to the contractor about her house.

The serious expression on Austin's face was not reassuring.

"Thanks Mark. I'll discuss the situation with the owner and get back to you." He closed his phone and glanced at her.

"What's wrong?" she asked.

"Did you buy the house from a Realtor?" he asked.

"No, I bought it directly from the owner. Why?"

"The wiring isn't up to code. And the water damage from your neighbor's fire means you also need to replace the dry wall in the right-hand corner of the living room." His expression was grim. "It's going to take a few weeks to get your house into shape before you and Josh can move back in."

Stunned, she sat down in the closest kitchen

chair. Surely he was exaggerating. "Weeks?" she echoed.

"Lindsey, I'd like to help. I don't want to steal your independence, but I need to know you and Josh are safe. Plus, it's obvious Josh could really use a good male role model right now to help keep him in school." He caught her hands in his, his gaze imploring. "Will you, please, consider moving in with me? At least until your house repairs are complete?"

CHAPTER FOUR

"MOVE in with you?" Lindsey stared at him, hardly able to comprehend what he was saying. Move in with Austin? So the two of them would be together all the time? Did he have any idea what he was asking of her? She pushed out of his grip, trying to rein in her turbulent emotions. "No. I'm sorry, but I can't."

"Why not?" Austin didn't get angry or upset, but looked truly puzzled. "Are you afraid I'll get in your way?" An odd expression flickered across his face. "Are you seeing someone?"

"What?" She almost burst out laughing and quickly covered the strangled sound with a cough. "No. Heavens, no. I'm not remotely interested in seeing anyone." Bad enough to realize she was attracted to him.

"Then why won't you let me help?" Austin's brows drew together in a frown. "This is what friends are for, to support each other in difficult times."

Lindsey sighed. Friends. He'd been Sam's friend, not really hers. Sure they'd chatted when they'd bumped into each other at work, but it wasn't as if they'd had deeply personal conversations or anything. How could she think of Austin as a friend, when every moment she was with him she was so aware of him as a man? Impossible. She lifted her chin. "If I were a guy, you wouldn't be inviting me to move in with you. But because I'm a helpless female with a young son, then I must need your support, right?"

Austin was quiet for a long moment. "Lindsey, you couldn't be further from the truth. I don't see you as a helpless female at all. You're a wonderful, smart, caring emergency nurse. I respect you more than I can say. But think about Josh for a minute. He's obviously going through some difficult times. I got him to open up a little just now, and he is having trouble coping with Sam's death. Don't you think staying here for a little while might be better for him?"

She opened her mouth to argue and then closed it again, without uttering a word. He'd effectively pointed out the weakness she couldn't argue against. Josh would always come first with her. She was thrilled he'd opened up to Austin. Maybe her son did need a male role model right now. If she was honest, she knew she couldn't find a better guy for the job than Austin.

Still, she wavered. Hadn't her mother often used the same excuse? *We need to move in with Richard because we can't afford to pay our rent. I'm doing this for you, Lindsey. Trust me, I know what I'm doing.*

"No strings, Lindsey," Austin was saying, as if reading her thoughts. "I swear to you, I only want to help. Why don't you try staying here, just for a week or so, and see how it goes? If you don't like it, I'll help you move into a hotel."

And he would. Deep in her heart she knew that much. If she insisted on going to a hotel, he'd take her. Logically, she knew Austin wasn't like all those men her mother had hooked up with after her father had taken off, leaving them with a heavy mortgage, not unlike the debts Sam had left her. The men her mother had married hadn't been horribly abusive or anything, her mother hadn't been that far gone, but moving in with one guy after another had been difficult.

Ten years ago she'd thought Sam had been so different. As it had turned out, he had been more like her father than she'd ever realized. Which only made her that much more determined not to be like her mother.

"I don't know, Austin," she hedged, wishing she had another option. The memory of the Tollivers' fire hadn't dimmed from her mind. As much as she wanted to be independent, she wasn't willing to put her son's safety at risk. If

Austin said the wiring wasn't up to code, she believed him. "I'm worried about how this may affect Josh. I don't want him to think we're, well..." She trailed off, embarrassed. "He'll look to you as a surrogate father and I don't want him to be lost all over again when we have to move back home," she amended.

"Lindsey, I'm not about to drop out of Josh's life, no matter where you decide to live." Austin's gaze captured hers. "I'd like to stay involved if you'll let me, as a big brother."

His idea was logical. Tempting. Could she do this? Could she live with Austin while keeping her attraction a secret?

This wasn't about her, but about Josh. She could suffer through anything for Josh's sake.

Hoping she wasn't taking the easy way out, she slowly nodded. "All right, Austin. I'll agree to a trial period to see how things go. But I'd like you to try to get them to rush the repairs on my house, OK?"

"Sure." Relief flooded his features and he

grinned. "Thanks, Lindsey. You won't regret this, I promise."

His brilliantly white grin did funny things to her stomach. She managed a weak smile in return, hoping he was right.

But deep down she suspected she might look back at this moment with regret.

While Austin and Josh went to see Dr Sandberg, Lindsey busied herself with making dinner. She didn't go crazy trying to impress Austin with her culinary talents, but threw together a simple spaghetti meal.

Still, she felt a warm glow when Austin sniffed the air with obvious appreciation when they got back. "Wow. Something smells great."

"It's no big deal." She tried to downplay the domesticity of the moment, although she felt the intimacy keenly. "Like you said yesterday, I had to make something for Josh, and made enough for you, too."

"Thanks." His simple acceptance helped make

her feel less self-conscious. This living-together stuff was going to take some getting used to.

The three of them sat down at the table, and she was pleased when Austin took the time to explain their situation to Josh.

"Your house sustained a fair amount of water damage after your neighbor's fire," Austin said, looking directly at Josh. "I hope you don't mind, but I convinced your mom that the two of you should stay here for a while, until after the repairs are completed."

"Really?" Josh's bright blue eyes, so much like Sam's, flashed with hope. "That would be so cool!"

"It's a temporary arrangement, Josh," she warned. "A couple of weeks at the most."

"I know," he agreed readily enough. She suspected a couple of weeks seemed like forever to a nine-year-old. "I can't wait to tell Tony!"

As Tony lived just a few blocks away, she understood his enthusiasm. For a moment she felt reassured by her decision. Maybe these few weeks wouldn't be so bad. Anything to help turn

Josh around from the stranger he'd been to the boy she'd once known.

"Lindscy, I was thinking that it would be good for Josh to learn Tai Kwon Do."

"What?" She paused, her fork halfway to her mouth as she swung her gaze back to Austin. "Are you crazy? How exactly does learning Tai Kwon Do teach Josh not to skip school?" She was seriously annoyed. Why on earth had he brought this up right in front of Josh? Had Austin done it on purpose, so that she could be the bad guy when she had to say no?

He was interfering in her life again.

"Actually, Tai Kwon Do is all about self-discipline, which is a trait that can be applied to many things, like homework." Austin finished his spaghetti, and then surprised her by standing and clearing away the dirty dishes. "The whole focus of the martial arts is all about teaching kids self-control."

Oh, sure. She was supposed to believe that? At her obvious skepticism, he continued, "Seriously,

Lindsey, I wouldn't have suggested it if I didn't think it would help. In fact, I ran the idea past Dr Sandberg and she thought it would be good for Josh, too. And you don't have to worry about the cost—consider this an early birthday present from me to Josh."

"Please, Mom?" Josh's gaze implored her to agree. "I promise I won't skip school anymore."

She sighed, glancing between the two of them, wondering if she was the one being unreasonable. She wanted to refuse on principle, because Austin was interfering again. Especially as taking Austin's money for something like this went against the grain.

Yet hadn't she asked for Austin's help when Josh had skipped school? What if she was wrong? If Dr Sandberg had given permission, this could be just what Josh needed. When was the last time she'd seen Josh look so excited?

Months. Since before Sam's funeral.

Wavering, she slowly nodded. "I'll consider it, Josh, but you need to know, if you skip school or get into another argument with other kids on the playground, I'll yank you out of those classes so fast, your head will spin."

"Yay! Thanks, Mom." Following Austin's example, Josh picked up his empty plate and carried it to the sink.

"Finish your homework," Austin said in a stern tone.

Josh nodded and ran back to his room. For a moment she was irritated with Austin for his seemingly effortless ability to get her son to listen.

Then was ashamed of herself for resenting him. After all, wasn't the need for a father figure exactly why she'd agreed to this arrangement? She should be grateful Austin cared enough about Josh to be there for him.

"Thanks, Lindsey," Austin said softly. "I think learning Tai Kwon Do is just what Josh needs to give him some badly needed self-confidence."

"I hope so," she said, carrying her own dishes over to the sink. "Although next time you'd better run the idea past me first, without involving Josh. I didn't appreciate being put on the spot like that."

Austin winced at her sharp tone and looked apologetic as he took the dirty plate from her hands. "Sorry about that. You're right. I guess I didn't think." He shooed her away from the sink. "You cooked, so it's my job to clean up. Why don't you relax for a few minutes? Later on we can go back to your house to get the rest of your things."

Relax? While living in the same house as Austin? Not likely. "It's your night off," she protested. "Surely you have better things to do?"

"Nope." His tone was cheerful. "Why don't you make a list of whatever you think you'll need over the next few weeks? As soon as I'm finished here, we'll get going."

She couldn't think of anything they'd need. Austin pretty much had everything covered in his house. As she sat at the table, watching him work, she belatedly realized that her decision to move in with Austin might cramp his bachelor lifestyle. Hadn't he point-blank asked her if she was seeing someone? Just because she wasn't interested in a relationship, it didn't mean Austin wasn't. After all, this was his night off. What if he wanted to go out tonight?

What if he met some woman he wanted to bring home? To spend the night with?

A pang of jealousy cramped her stomach, making her feel sick.

"I realize you probably have plans on your nights off, so don't worry about us," she said quickly, pushing aside the lump in her throat. "Josh is usually in bed by nine o'clock on school nights and I'm usually asleep early, too, so you don't have to worry about disturbing us or anything." She knew she was babbling but couldn't seem to stop. "I mean, really, don't think Josh and I will get in the way of your…uh…social life. Just pretend we're not here."

Austin paused in the act of rinsing the dishes and neatly stacking them in the dishwasher to glance at her. "Lindsey, I'm not seeing anyone and haven't for months. Do you honestly think I'd bring some woman home with you and Josh here?"

He hadn't seen anyone for months? Secretly relieved, she shrugged. "Why not? You said yourself we're friends."

"We are, but I'm not interested in a social life, as you put it." His grin was lopsided. "Right now, nothing is more important than you and Josh."

"But if you change your mind—" she started.

He interrupted. "I won't."

"All right, then." She smiled back, a warm glow sweeping through her at his words, even though she knew he didn't really mean them.

At least, not in the way she wished he did.

That night, Austin couldn't sleep. He tossed and turned, kicking off the covers, unable to bear the cotton sheets against his body. He threw himself on his back, feeling as if his skin was too tight for his body. What in the hell was wrong with him? He hadn't felt this wired since the night of the fire.

After a few hours, he rolled out of bed and

doused himself in cold water, hoping the cool shower would ease the aching tension. It helped a little, but as he stared at his reflection in the mirror above the sink, he forced himself to admit the hard truth.

Sharing a house with Lindsey was going to be more difficult than he'd thought. Had he been nuts to open his home to her? If this was how bad he was after one night, he couldn't imagine how he'd feel after a few weeks.

Being this close to Lindsey without having her was going to drive him insane.

He sighed and rubbed the back of his neck. He'd just have to get over it. He'd had the ridiculous notion that focusing on Josh would help keep his desire for Lindsey under control. But Josh was old enough to spend a fair amount of time with his friends, and during those times Josh was gone or otherwise occupied, swimming in the pool out back or playing video games, he and Lindsey had been alone. And those stolen moments did nothing to help him ignore his growing attraction for her.

Turning away from his rueful reflection, he drew on a clean pair of boxers and stood at the patio doors, gazing out at the pool in the backyard, where Josh and Tony had spent a good couple of hours earlier that afternoon, playing water volleyball. At least Josh was enjoying himself in his new surroundings.

Too bad he couldn't say the same thing for himself.

Hell. If he thought going out and finding a willing woman to take the edge off would help to get rid of his obsession with Lindsey, he'd do it.

But during his most recent trip home, he'd learned that other women didn't hold the same appeal they once had. At first he'd thought it had been because he hadn't gotten over Sam's death. But then he'd realized it had been more than that. No matter how he'd tried, he hadn't been able to summon the smallest flicker of interest in the cute redhead he'd met one night or the sexy brunette he'd been introduced to the following night.

He simply wasn't interested in anyone else.

Only Lindsey.

And that scared the heck out of him.

Unable to bear the closed-in feel of his bedroom any longer, he turned away and crossed the room. Silently, he opened his door and padded down the hall, past Lindsey's and Josh's rooms, to the kitchen.

He knew his way around without using any lights, and his bare feet didn't make a sound as he entered the kitchen. But when he bumped into something soft, he abruptly realized he wasn't alone.

Lindsey let out a soft cry, taking a quick step backward. He reached out and grasped her shoulders to steady her.

"Gosh, you scared me," she said in a strangled whisper.

"I'm sorry," he said, immediately contrite. He did feel bad about frightening her, but he couldn't find any remorse over bumping into her like that. Even in the dark, she was the vision of his dreams, her hair falling in waves around her shoulders.

Her soft, lemony scent went straight to his groin, his body aroused to the point of pain.

Being this close to her only reinforced the edgy awareness he'd been battling all night.

She turned away, the flash of moonlight through the window bathing her profile in a soft glow. He sucked in a quick breath when he saw the glint of tears.

"What is it?" he asked quickly, tightening his grip on her slim shoulders. "What's wrong?"

"Nothing." Lindsey's denial was too quick, and she brushed away the tears, trying to turn away from him.

He didn't like the thought of her crying. "Lindsey, please, tell me what has upset you. Is it Josh? Something I said? Something I did? What?"

"No, it's nothing like that." This time, her lips curved in a small smile. "I…had a bad dream, that's all. Then when you scared me, it all came back. It's silly. Don't know why I let a dream get to me."

A bad dream he could handle, he thought—

although his heart still squeezed at the thought of her being so upset. He drew her against him, offering comfort. "Hey, it's OK. We've all had bad dreams at some point."

Expecting her to give him a brief hug then draw away, he was surprised when she surrendered to him, burying her face in the curve of his neck, hanging on as if she didn't plan to ever let go.

His heart thudded painfully in his chest and he slid a hand down the curve of her back, suddenly aware of how little she was wearing. The thin cotton T-shirt wasn't much of a barrier—he could feel the warmth of her skin radiating through it.

When her lips brushed lightly against his neck, he thought for a moment he'd imagined the caress. But his body tightened when the moisture of her breath fanned his cheek.

"Lindsey?" he murmured, mixed signals clamoring in his brain. Was it even remotely possible she wanted the same thing he did?

She tipped her head back to look up at him and

the silent offering was too much to ignore. He bent his head, covering her expectantly parted lips with his mouth, claiming her as his in a bone-jarring, mind-numbing kiss.

CHAPTER FIVE

AUSTIN'S kiss was so simmering hot Lindsay was surprised her feet didn't melt to the floor.

Rational thought vanished. She should push him away, but the need clamoring through her had other ideas. Instead, she clutched his shoulders and returned his kiss, basking in the thrill of desire. How long had it been since she'd kissed a man?

Aeons. Or so it seemed.

Austin didn't just kiss her, he made love to her with his mouth, as if nothing was more important than her lips.

And then suddenly he thrust her away from him, breathing deeply, and holding on to the kitchen counter for support. "I'm sorry, Lindsey. I had no right to cross the line like that."

Bereft, she leaned against the sink, her own knees threatening to buckle. Why had he stopped? She licked her lips, tasting him, and it took all her control not to throw herself back into his arms.

Bad enough that she'd practically begged for his kiss.

"Don't move out," Austin was saying now, talking fast as if he was worried she was going to interrupt. Did he think she was angry with him? A hysterical laugh nearly broke free. "I promise I won't cross the line this way ever again."

OK… Obviously he wanted to keep their relationship on friendship terms. She should be glad, because she wasn't in the market for anything more either. Yet there was an emptiness inside her where love and passion had once been. She swallowed hard and nodded, knowing he probably couldn't see her in the dark.

What if she wanted a kiss to happen again? What if she wanted more?

Forget it. What she wanted didn't matter. Austin

was a friend. Maybe he was trying to protect her from ending up as a one-night stand. Obviously he wasn't a guy who did long-term relationships.

At the moment a one-night stand didn't sound like such a bad thing. Anything to make this ache of longing go away.

"It's all right, Austin. I— Don't worry about it." What could she say? Admit that she'd wanted that toe-curling kiss as much as he had? And then what? She didn't think she could really handle a one-night stand, as tempting as it sounded. Austin wasn't the type of guy to settle down— he must have had ample opportunity over the past few years. She'd never met a steady girl-friend of his. There had to be a reason he avoided long-term relationships.

"You won't leave?" he asked again, his tone anxious.

"No," she said slowly. "I won't leave."

He was quiet for a moment, before murmuring, "Good. Thank you. Good night, Lindsey. Sweet dreams."

"Good night." Unable to move, she stayed where she was, until Austin padded silently back down the hall to his bedroom. Alone again, she let out a heavy sigh and sank into the nearest kitchen chair, willing her heart to return to its normal rhythm.

She really should leave. Should pack up her own and Josh's things and move into the nearest hotel. But she couldn't. Because truthfully she couldn't afford a hotel. And Josh needed Austin.

Instead, she vowed to find the strength to keep a safe distance between them.

Lindsey managed to keep out of Austin's way over the next few days. Of course, it helped that Austin seemed to be staying away from her, too.

And while it hurt a bit to realize he was avoiding her, she told herself to get over it. It was better this way.

The one time they were forced to talk to each other was during dinner. They'd gotten into the habit of sharing their evening meal each night in a very familylike way. Except Austin insisted on taking turns with the cooking, depending on which of them happened to get home first. On certain days, like tonight, he drove Josh and his friend Tony to their Tai Kwon Do lesson, so she'd gotten home before he did. She didn't mind cooking for him. And tonight, when he and Josh walked in, she decided it was past time they had a serious discussion about the progress on her house. She'd left the details for Austin to deal with for too long.

"Something smells delicious," he greeted her with a cheerful grin.

She rolled her eyes. He always said that, no matter if she made tuna casserole or lasagna. Tonight she'd thrown together baked chicken. Nothing fancy.

"Thanks. Have a seat, it's ready." She waited until everyone was seated and digging into their meals before getting to the point of what she wanted to know. "Austin, you never told me exactly what the repairs would be on my house. I need to know how much this is all going to cost."

His brow rose. "Don't worry about it, I'll take care of everything."

She ground her teeth at his slightly condescending tone. "It's my house, remember? I'd like to know exactly what is being done and how much it will cost."

He paused as if finally realizing she was dead serious, and then slowly nodded. "All right, I'll get you the paperwork after we finish eating."

Slightly mollified, she took a bite of her chicken. Not bad, if she did say so herself.

"Mom, we learned how to do a jumping snap kick today," Josh jumped in with an excited voice. "You should see how high I can kick! I can't wait until we get to break boards with our feet."

She couldn't help but smile. "I'm glad you're enjoying your lessons."

"Will you come and watch when I test out to become a yellow belt?" Josh persisted.

She didn't realize testing out was part of the

process. Sliding a questioning glance over to Austin, she saw him give a slight nod. "Sure. I'd love to."

"It won't be for a few weeks yet, but I can't wait. White belts are for sissies."

"Hey, don't talk like that." Austin spoke up. "Remember what your sensei said? There will always be someone worse than you and better than you. This is a test of your own strength and endurance, not anyone else's. You're only competing against yourself."

"Yeah, I know." Josh made a wry face.

She was glad to see her son was excited about his classes and hoped this would channel his energy into something constructive rather than destructive, like skipping school. The one nice thing about Josh's classes was that they were right after school, so with Austin's help driving him on his days off she'd been able to sign up for a couple of extra shifts on the days Josh had class.

It sounded like she was going to need every dime she could make in order to pay for the repairs.

After Austin had cleaned up the dinner dishes, he brought a stack of papers over to the kitchen table. "Here are the quotes I've received and obviously I've accepted the most reasonable ones. The electricians are rewiring the house first, and then I'll arrange for the drywall repairs."

Steeling herself for the worst, she still let out a horrified gasp when she saw the amount of both the wiring and the drywall repairs. "That much?"

Austin nodded. "I'm afraid so. But I'm pretty sure your home owner's insurance should cover the bulk of the cost."

She blinked, thinking she'd imagined those extra zeros on the end of the number, but she hadn't. How in the world would she manage to pay that amount? She didn't have enough equity in the house to take out a second mortgage.

And thanks to Sam, her credit rating wasn't all that great. Although she'd made certain every single one of his debts had been paid off in full, by selling the house and using most of his life insurance policy. All she had left was a small nestegg, which didn't come close to covering the cost of the repairs.

She stared at the amount, feeling foolish. Why hadn't she realized sooner how much this was going to cost? Mortified at the thought of asking Austin for a loan, she stared at her hands. There had to be another way.

"Lindsey?" Austin reached out and took her hand. It was the first time he'd touched her since that moment of moonlight madness they'd shared in the kitchen. A kiss that had haunted her ever since. "What's wrong?"

She had to tell him. As much as she wanted to crawl under a rock and hide, she'd learned the hard way that ignoring her problems would not make them go away.

"I don't have home owner's insurance." She couldn't bring herself to meet his gaze. "But don't worry, I'll head over to the bank first thing in the morning to see if I can take out a loan."

"You don't have home owner's insurance?" Austin repeated in surprise. "You did get

Sam's life insurance payout after he died, didn't you?"

"Yes." She was embarrassed to tell him just how badly Sam had gotten them into debt. Especially as she'd been so clueless. Why hadn't she insisted on being involved in paying their bills? Sam used to get so upset when she'd tried to help, she'd simply backed off. And she'd almost done the same thing again with the repairs on her house, leaving everything to Austin. Why hadn't she learned from her mistakes? "You must have figured out things have been difficult financially. But it doesn't matter." She forced herself to look him in the eye. "It's my house, Austin. I'll pay for the repairs. Thanks for arranging all the contractors for me." She tugged her hand out of his, and stood.

"Lindsey, wait—" he started.

But she walked out, leaving him alone, not wanting to see the flash of pity in his eyes.

Austin couldn't believe things had gotten so desperate for Lindsey and Josh. What in the heck had Sam done? She'd said she'd gotten the life insurance payout but, still, somehow she'd been forced to sell her house.

Thank heavens he'd managed to convince her to move in for a while. At least he could help cover the cost of her grocery bills. And using the Tai Kwon Do classes as a birthday present for Josh had been pure genius. He hadn't minded paying for the sessions, along with the V-necked *dobak* Josh wore with pride.

He scrubbed his hands over his face. During the day he managed to keep busy enough to stay out of Lindsey's way. He'd wanted her for so long, but first she'd belonged to Sam and now she was still grieving over Sam's death. No matter how he tried to talk himself out of wanting her, the nights were pure torture. He couldn't forget their kiss, the burning memory lingering.

He'd crossed the line—had allowed his stupid testosterone-laden desires to ruin their friendship. And he found he really missed their easy camaraderie. He'd berated himself over and over again for losing control, for allowing his physical desire to override his common sense.

Yet, no matter what, he couldn't forget that she hadn't been the one to break off the embrace that she'd started. What would have happened if he hadn't stopped? He hadn't imagined the way she'd kissed him back.

Unless she'd pretended he had been Sam? Refusing to delve into that grim possibility, he made his way to the fire station.

"Hey, Monroe. How are you?" Jack Nelson, one of his fellow paramedics, greeted him when he walked in. "Did you have a good couple of days off?"

"Yeah, did you?" Jack would have been surprised to know his time had been spent centered around a nine-year-old kid, but he didn't bother to elaborate. A lot of the guys, especially the married ones with families, automatically assumed he lived the wild, single-guy lifestyle. But the sad truth was that he hadn't been out with a woman in months.

Since Sam's death.

Since realizing how completely hung up he was on his best friend's widow.

"Have things been quiet?" Austin asked, as they made their way into the kitchen. When the guys weren't fighting fires or responding to para-medic calls, they liked to eat.

Following his nose, he realized they were in for a treat. Thank heavens, Big Joe Johnson was already cooking up a hearty breakfast feast.

"Pretty quiet. A few routine paramedic runs. No fire calls, though." Jack sounded disappointed.

Californians knew their sunny, warm and dry weather predisposed them to fires. As much as a firefighter didn't want to see people suffer trag-edies, there was something in them that longed for the adrenaline rush of fighting a fire. Heck, it was one of the reasons he'd tried out for the smoke jumping crew. He liked knowing his talents were needed.

"Hungry?" Big Joe called out, waving a spatula at them. "It's almost ready."

"I could eat," Austin said, taking a seat at the table. It was a good thing there was a weight room in the back, otherwise they'd grow fat and lazy from Big Joe's meals.

Although Lindsey's dinners were a pretty close second. In fact, he looked forward to going home, knowing she was there.

Shying away from that dangerous thought, he listened as the guys argued over the latest sports games. They'd finished eating when the first call came in. Since Austin and Jack were the freshest of the bunch, they were identified as the first responders.

"What do we have?" Austin asked from the driver's seat.

"Sixty-four-year-old unconscious man with a history of heart problems," Jack repeated what the dispatcher had told him.

"He fell?"

"Not that we know of."

Austin pulled up in front of the patient's house. His wife was waiting anxiously for them in the doorway. "This way," she urged, leading the way into the bedroom.

Carrying his EMS pack on his back, Austin followed her. "What sorts of heart problems does he have?" Austin asked.

"He had a heart attack about a year ago." The patient's wife pulled out a handwritten note as they entered the room, where the patient was still lying in bed. "Here are the medications he's on."

"Smart of you to write them down." Austin took the list and set it on the bedside table. He began a quick assessment, glad the guy was breathing, if barely. "Give him a little oxygen."

Jack pulled out an oxygen mask, and placed it over the patient's nose and mouth. The guy groaned a little, indicating he wasn't as unconscious as Austin had originally thought. Austin quickly connected the patient to their portable heart monitor and then obtained a blood pressure.

"BP low, 96 over 70, and he's in sinus tach with a rate of 148." Austin glanced at the medication list again. "He takes a beta-blocker, aspirin and wears a nitroglycerine patch."

"We'd better get the patch off with his blood pressure so low." Jack opened the guy's shirt and removed it.

"Does he have any other medical problems?" Austin asked the hovering wife.

"He's diabetic, but doesn't take any pills or insulin. He just watches his diet."

"Check the blood-glucose level," Austin advised. The guy's vitals weren't great, but they were stable enough for transport. "I'll start an IV."

"Sounds good." Jack pulled out the tiny glucometer and proceeded to get the glucose results while Austin inserted the antecubital IV. While he worked, the wife explained how her husband had been sick with a cold for several days, staying in bed longer than normal. He'd just never bounced back.

After a few seconds the tiny machine beeped. "Holy cow, his glucose is 750," Jack announced.

"He must be in DKA, diabetic ketoacidosis," Austin murmured, as he hung a bag of normal saline. In the course of his paramedic career, he'd seen lots of patients in a similar condition. "Let's get him to the hospital."

With Jack's help, he lifted the patient onto the gurney. The closest treatment center was Sun Valley Community Hospital, so once they were in the ambulance he radioed the dispatcher to relay a message for their arrival.

The ED was expecting them, and he wasn't completely surprised to see Lindsey was the nurse waiting to take the patient. In fact, if he was honest, he'd admit he had been hoping to run into her there.

Either at work or at home, seeing Lindsey was the highlight of his day.

Austin rattled off the patient's vitals and glucose level as they transferred him to the ED cart.

"How much fluid did you give him?" Lindsey asked with a frown.

"Only a few hundred cc's." He glanced at her,

trying to gauge why she was asking. "With his cardiac history, I didn't want to risk heart failure."

"I understand." She flashed him a small smile. "I just don't smell any ketones on his breath and it makes me wonder if he really has DKA or something more serious, like hyperosmolar, hyperglycemic non-ketotic coma."

He stared at her in surprise. "What's the difference?"

"Profound dehydration causes HHNK. You said he's a diet-controlled diabetic, right?" Austin nodded, impressed with her knowledge. "We'll know more as soon as we get some lab results back." She took the tube of blood she'd just drawn and handed it to a lab tech. "But in HHNK, the patient usually has enough insulin in their body to prevent ketoacidosis, but not enough to allow the body to use glucose. These patients are often much sicker than they look. HHNK is often misdiagnosed."

The doctor walked into the room. "What do we have?"

Austin stood to the side, listening as Lindsey ran down the patient's history and current vitals. The guy's blood pressure hadn't improved, even after Jack had removed the nitro patch.

"Run a twelve-lead and then increase his fluids," Dr Graff ordered. "Call me as soon as you get those lab results back."

"I will." Lindsey called the EKG tech over.

Austin knew there was no reason to stay, other than his very personal need to know exactly what the diagnosis was. He'd made an assumption and it bothered him to think it might have been the wrong one. "Jack, let's hang out for a few minutes."

"No problem." Jack glanced around. "I wouldn't mind a cup of coffee, though."

"In the break room," Lindsey said, jerking her thumb over her shoulder in the general direction of the staff lounge.

Jack rambled off but Austin stayed right where he was. "How long does it take for the chemistry results to come back?"

"Should be any time now—they're usually

pretty quick." Lindsey glanced at him. "What's wrong? You look worried."

He lifted a shoulder. "Maybe we should have treated him differently. The wife did say he hadn't been feeling well for a couple of days."

"Hey, normally, you wouldn't give a sixty-four-year-old a megadose of fluids, especially with a cardiac history," Lindsey assured him. "You did the right thing."

He appreciated her staunch support. This was exactly what he'd always admired about her. She never made the paramedic crew feel like second-class citizens.

"Lindsey? Call from the lab on line three."

She hurried off and he watched as she wrote down the various lab results. When she returned, she handed him the slip of paper. "Definitely HHNK. See? Ketones are negative."

He nodded, handing the slip back. "So now what?"

Lindsey was already picking up the phone, calling Dr Graff. Austin listened as she relayed the information, and then took more orders. She hung up the phone. "He's going to be admitted to the ICU."

"Good." He tucked his hands in his pockets, reassured that his and Jack's treatment hadn't been too far off the mark. "Thanks for letting me know."

"You're welcome." She hurried back to the patient, and he glanced around for Jack. Was the guy still guzzling coffee in the staff lounge? He went back and found his partner. As they finished the details of their paperwork, he explained what Lindsey had taught him about their patient's illness.

Once Jack had dropped off the final copy of their report, they headed out to the ambulance.

Austin was about to slide into the driver's seat when he stopped, realizing he'd forgotten to tell Lindsey that there was an extra Tai Kwon Do class that evening for Josh. As he was working, she'd have to take him. Instead of calling her later, he decided he'd better tell her now. "Here." He tossed Jack the keys. "I'll be right back."

"Sure." Jack brightened at the chance to drive.

He headed back inside, glancing around for Lindsey. Their patient was gone so she must have transported the guy up to the ICU already.

How long would it take? he wondered, glancing at his watch. Curious, he walked to the staff lounge, intending to ask. He was surprised to find Lindsey chatting with Mary, one of the other nurses.

"He's just a friend," Lindsey was saying. "You know his reputation around here as well as I do."

"Yeah, but people can change," Mary pointed out. "Maybe if you gave him a chance, he could be more than a friend."

"Austin? More than a friend? Never." Lindsey's firm voice stopped him in his tracks. "I could never be interested in a guy like him."

CHAPTER SIX

AUSTIN wished he could duck back out of the lounge without being seen, but at that moment the nurse Lindsey had been talking to made eye contact.

Wasn't there some saying about people who eavesdropped never hearing good things about themselves? Too true.

Forcing himself to brazen it out, he stepped further into the room. "Lindsey?" At the sound of his voice she jumped around, her eyes going wide and her cheeks flushed pink with embarrassment. "I forgot to mention, Josh has an extra Tai Kwon Do lesson tonight. You'll need to pick him up at four."

"Oh. Um…OK. Thanks for letting me know." Her obvious distress tugged at him.

He flashed a reassuring smile, although he still felt hurt by her comments. "No problem. Have a good day. See you tomorrow."

"Sure. Take care."

Leaving the staff lounge, he headed back out to where Jack was waiting in the ambulance. As his partner drove back to the station, he replayed her comment over and over again in his mind. She wasn't interested in a guy like him. Although he'd vowed to stay away from her, the comment rankled. He shouldn't take it personally, he knew he had a bit of a reputation because he'd dated so many different women. The truth of the matter was that he'd never found the woman he was looking for.

It wasn't until late into his shift that he realized Lindsey hadn't mentioned anything about avoiding relationships because she was still in love with Sam.

He knew she had to be grieving over losing her husband. He was nuts to even think about waiting around for the time she might get over Sam enough to start dating again.

But if that day ever came, would she consider giving him a chance?

He wasn't sure but he was willing to wait to find out.

After that mortifying experience in the staff lounge, Lindsey was relieved she didn't have to face Austin until the next day. She couldn't believe he'd overheard her thoughtless comment. Austin did have a reputation with women, especially as he'd dated half the staff in the Sun Valley ED. But she shouldn't have been so harsh.

It had been the only way she could think of to get Mary's thoughts out of her head, though. Because she was attracted enough without Mary putting ideas into her head.

Austin arrived home moments after Josh left for school the next morning, yawning widely, his bloodshot eyes betraying his exhaustion.

"Bad night?" Lindsay asked with sympathy.

"Busy." He lifted a negligent shoulder. "Nothing too horrible, just a lot of routine calls. Enough to keep us hopping all night, though."

"Get some sleep," she advised.

"I will." He glanced at her, belatedly noting her scrubs. "Are you working again today?"

She'd picked up an extra shift, looking for some additional money. Especially as the bank hadn't yet promised her a loan. "Yes. I'll be home by four, though. Call me if you need me to pick Josh up."

"I'll get him." Austin hesitated, as if he wanted to say something more. An awkward silence fell and it was on the tip of her tongue to apologize for being so blunt but then the moment passed as he bade her good-night and headed down to his room.

"Good night." Lindsey watched him disappear through the doorway, ridiculously tempted to follow him. What was wrong with her anyway? Austin wasn't the type of guy she should be attracted to. And not just because he dated a different woman every night.

Austin was a smoke jumper. A risk-taker. An adrenaline junkie.

Even as she mentally compared him to Sam, she knew she wasn't being fair. Austin might like the thrill and excitement of being a smoke jumper, but he was different from Sam.

Her husband had used smoke jumping as an excuse to avoid her. To avoid the family responsibilities he'd begun to resent.

Not caring that his long absences only drove a deeper wedge between them.

Staring out of Austin's kitchen window, nursing a cup of coffee, Lindsey thought back over those months before Sam had tested out to be a smoke jumper. If she was honest, she'd admit her marriage had been in trouble even then. Before Sam had begun to stay away from home for long periods of time. Before he'd gotten so far into debt. Maybe he had been partially right when he'd accused her of driving him away.

Maybe she had been more at fault for the disintegration of their marriage than she'd been willing to admit.

Lindsey's shift started slowly, but soon patients were streaming in. When the EMT crew brought in a drunk driver who'd crashed his car into a street-pole, she was reminded of her problems with Sam all over again.

Luckily, the patient, named Frank Jones, wasn't seriously injured. A gash across his forehead would need a few stitches, but otherwise Frank was remarkably unhurt.

She shouldn't be surprised, considering Frank's alcohol level was twice the legal limit. He'd admitted to having a couple of martinis. What had reminded her of Sam, though, had been when he'd claimed he was upset because his wife had announced she was leaving him.

She thought about the night before Sam had left for his smoke jumping mission. She'd told him she was filing for divorce, too. There had been a part of her that had thought he wouldn't care anyway as he'd spent more time away from her than at home.

But he had cared, or so he'd claimed. And then he'd died.

Uncomfortable with the memories, Lindsey concentrated on Frank's minor injuries. She started an IV, giving him plenty of fluids to help counteract the effects of the alcohol, and even fed him lunch.

Toward the end of her shift Dr Delaney cleared Frank for discharge. She watched as the police took him away in handcuffs, arresting him for driving under the influence. Frank had been totally dejected, telling her that for sure now his wife wouldn't give him a second chance.

If Sam hadn't died, would they have tried to make their marriage work? She'd thought long and hard about even filing for divorce, but the empty marriage hadn't been what she had wanted out of life. There had to be more to a marriage, a partnership, than simple coexistence.

Still, it wasn't as if Sam had been a bad guy. They'd gotten married too young, when she'd discovered herself to be pregnant with Josh. And somehow, over the years, the love between them had evaporated until there had been nothing left.

She wished she had someone to talk to about her marriage. Someone who would understand her dilemma. Austin? She bit her lip uncertainly.

Why not? Maybe it would be easier to view Austin as a friend if she started to treat him like one. Maybe if he knew what had really happened in her marriage, some of the attraction between them would fade. Love from afar was always easier than dealing with the reality of every day.

On her way home from work, Lindsey stopped by her house to pick up the mail. She'd forgotten to go to the post office to temporarily change her mailing address to Austin's.

There were a few bills, but payment wasn't late as she'd arranged for electronic payments directly out of her checking account. It was one way to repair her crippled credit rating.

There was an envelope from Josh's school. Progress report? With a sense of dread she drove home, trying to prepare for the worst.

Josh's grades had slipped over the past quarter. His poor grades, along with his truancy, had been signs that she was losing him. In the week they'd been living with Austin, things had seemed better. Yet maybe it was wishful thinking? A week was only seven days. How much influence could Austin really have made in such a short time?

Entering Austin's house quietly so she wouldn't wake him up, she carried the mail into the kitchen. Taking a deep breath, she opened the envelope and read Josh's progress report.

A heavy weight rolled off her chest. A couple of Cs but more As and Bs than she'd ever seen on his report card before. Much better than the last progress report she'd received.

She was grinning like an idiot when Austin

walked into the kitchen, wearing a T-shirt and pair of athletic shorts, his hair damp from a recent shower. He was up earlier than she'd expected and Josh didn't need to be picked up for another thirty minutes or so.

"Good news?" he asked, as he opened the fridge and poured himself a large glass of orange juice.

"Very good news." She waved the grades at him. "Josh's progress report. He's doing much better in school."

"Really?" Austin actually looked interested as he reached for the report, shutting the fridge door with his elbow as he scanned it with a quick eye. "Wow. They are good. I'm glad."

"Me, too." She knew much of this was a debt she owed to Austin. "You were right, Austin. Temporarily moving in with you and starting him in Tai Kwon Do classes seems to have made a huge difference. Thank you."

"You don't have to thank me," he protested. His compelling green gaze met hers. "I care about you and Josh. I'm happy to help."

She knew he meant it. If only Sam had felt the same way. At least before their marriage had crumbled. Ridiculous tears threatened, and she changed the subject to prevent from getting maudlin. "Maybe we should go out to dinner tonight to celebrate."

"Great idea." He flashed a lopsided smile. "But do we have to let Josh pick the place? We're likely to end up at some pizza joint if we do."

She had to laugh at his rueful expression. "Yeah, I know. But they are his grades after all."

"I guess." He stared at her and suddenly the kitchen seemed too small. Or maybe it was just the memory of their kiss that made her hyperaware of him.

"Well." She cleared her throat to cover the awkward moment. "If you're sure you're up to a night out, I'll pick up Josh and meet you back here in a bit."

"I can do it," he protested quickly. "You just walked in the door from work. Why don't you relax? Josh may have some homework to finish first anyway before we're ready to go."

His caring attitude was so novel, so nice, she couldn't refuse. "All right. Thanks."

"I'll see if I can talk Josh out of a pizza place on the way home," he added with a quick grin.

She laughed as he left, thinking how odd it was that Austin, the guy who'd never been married or had children of his own, managed to share the parenting duties more fairly than her husband ever had.

A trait which made him twice as attractive.

Austin hadn't been able to talk Josh out of a pizza celebration, but he did agree to Josh's request to bring Tony along for the celebration.

He'd wanted to take Lindsey to a nice restaurant for a change. Instead, they were headed to a popular pizza place with a small arcade attached.

When he saw Lindsey in the kitchen, wearing a gauzy skirt that swept her ankles, paired with a matching spaghetti-strap camisole top, he fought a surge of desire.

She was so beautiful. Sexy, without even trying.

Hell. Maybe it was a good thing they were going to a noisy pizza place. Anything more intimate and he might make a total fool out of himself, claiming her for his own.

The possessive need to have Lindsey belong to him caught him off guard. Since when had his deep physical attraction for her morphed into something more? But ever since he'd overheard her comment about his reputation, the idea wouldn't leave him alone.

Would she look at him differently if she knew his playboy days were over? Would she be willing to give him a chance if she knew how much he cared for her?

How he was beginning to fall in love with her?

Josh and Tony kept up a steady stream of conversation in the backseat as they headed to the restaurant. Once inside, they placed their order for large pizzas, loaded with everything Josh and Tony liked to eat. Then the boys disappeared into the arcade, leaving the adults alone.

"How was your day?" he asked, when the boys had left.

She shrugged. "It was all right. One of my patients was a drunk driver who'd crashed into a streetlight."

He levered his brow. "Drinking at noon, huh?"

Lindsey's smile was strained. "Yeah, well, it seems he was trying to drown his sorrows as his wife had just announced she was leaving him."

"I see." Her pensive gaze tugged at him. Something about this particular patient seemed to have gotten to her.

"Austin, have you given up smoke jumping?"

Her abrupt question surprised him. He sipped his soft drink, trying to figure out how to answer her. "I'm not sure. I went back right after our, uh, argument, but all I could think about was how Sam had died. I think I went back too soon." He lifted one shoulder and grimaced. "To be honest, I don't know if I'll ever be ready to go back."

She frowned, drawing imaginary patterns on the table with her fingertip. "It was my fault, you know."

Was she talking about Sam's death? "What? Lindsey, how could you possibly be at fault? You were hundreds of miles away when he died." He was the one who'd caused Sam's death, not her.

She stared at the tabletop, her voice so quiet he had to strain to hear. "I'm sure Sam mentioned we were having a few…problems."

"No, actually, he didn't." Austin frowned. Why hadn't Sam mentioned their problems? Maybe because, like most guys, talking about all that personal stuff wasn't easy. He tried to reassure her. "Hey, most marriages have their ups and downs, Lindsey. I'm sure your problems were similar to those in many other marriages."

She sat back, rubbing her hands over her arms as if she were cold, and slowly shook her head. "No. They were more serious than that."

"Serious?" He didn't know what to say. Sam had never breathed a word about any problems. "What happened? Did he do something to you? What?"

"No, nothing like that." Lindsey's expression turned even more grim. "Sam spent so much time away from home it seemed there was nothing left. No marriage. Nothing."

He blew out a breath, realizing what she was saying. The competition to become a smoke jumper was fierce. Only the best of the best made the crew. He and Sam had both been honored to be chosen. But the lengthy stints away from home, up to three months at a time, were hell on relationships. And suddenly he was cross with Sam. What had his buddy been thinking, to put a stupid job ahead of his wife and son?

He reached for her, capturing her tiny hands in his. "I understand, Lindsey. It's not your fault."

"No, I don't think you do understand," she countered, trying to tug her hands from his. "Don't you see? His death really was my fault.

I filed for divorce, Austin. Right before you guys were called up for that fire, I filed for divorce and told Sam he needed to move out."

CHAPTER SEVEN

AUSTIN tightened his grip on her hands and leaned forward, his gaze intense. "Lindsey, there's something you need to know…"

Josh and Tony came running back to their table before he could explain what had really happened the night Sam had died. The details he should have told her a long time ago. "Mom! Tony and I each won a game. Do you have any more quarters? We need to stay long enough for a tiebreaker! Otherwise how will we know who won?"

Lindsey gave another subtle tug on her hands, and this time Austin reluctantly let her go. She seemed flustered as she ran her fingers through her hair. "Maybe later, Josh. Right now, I think they're bringing our pizzas."

Sure enough, their server approached their table with two large pizzas and several soft drinks on her tray. She set everything out on the table, the kids barely waiting for her to move out of the way before digging eagerly into the food. Josh seemed happy, considering the way his mouth was stuffed with cheese and gooey pizza sauce.

Austin didn't mind when the rest of the evening centered around Josh, but he kept hearing Lindsey's words echoing in his head.

She'd been planning to divorce Sam. She'd asked Sam to move out of the house. The night he'd kissed her in his kitchen, she couldn't have been pretending he had been Sam if she'd been planning to divorce him.

Could she?

Probably not. Yet she'd clearly told her nurse friend that there was no way she could ever be interested in Austin as more than a friend.

Because of his reputation with women.

He watched her as she laughed at some story

Josh was telling and his gut clenched with need. She called to his senses the way no woman ever had. He'd always admired her, but now she was available. More so than he'd realized.

If he could convince her he'd given up his old ways, maybe he'd stand a chance.

He could face anything life threw at him, with Lindsey by his side.

Lindsey couldn't believe she'd bared her soul to Austin about her plans to divorce Sam.

She'd been carrying the secret for months.

Austin bantered with Josh and Tony as if he were an older brother. The boys seemed to enjoy having his undivided attention. Telling Austin the truth about her relationship with Sam had been cathartic. At least, now he knew that while she grieved over Sam's death, it wasn't the same grief she'd have felt if she'd still loved him.

The sad truth was that her love for Sam had died a long time ago.

And why it was so important for Austin to know that was something she didn't want to examine too closely.

After dinner, she watched with a mother's indulgence as the boys and Austin played one last tie-breaker video game, before they headed home. They dropped Tony off at his house along the way.

At Austin's house, Josh scrambled to get ready for bed. To keep busy, she folded a load of towels she'd tossed into the dryer, listening as Austin talked to her son.

"I'm proud of the way you've improved your grades and the way you've been staying in school," she heard Austin say. "Keep up the good work, Josh, OK?"

"I will. Actually, now that Tony and I are doing Tai Kwon Do, school doesn't seem so bad."

"Maybe it helps to think about something else besides losing your dad, huh?" Austin gave Josh's shoulder a gentle squeeze.

"Yeah. I still miss him, but I don't think about it all the time anymore," Josh agreed.

Lindsey paused in the middle of folding the last towel. She hadn't realized Josh had skipped school mostly because of missing his dad. Her heart ached for her son and she wished there was something more she could do for him.

But sometimes grief needed to run its course.

She finished folding the last towel and then walked down the hall toward Josh's bedroom. "All set? Did you brush your teeth?"

"Yep. See?" Josh bared his teeth for her, and then turned to Austin. "Good night, Austin."

"Good night, Josh."

She followed her son into his room, waiting until he crawled into bed before sitting on the edge. "I'm proud of you for staying in school, too, you know."

"Thanks Mom." Thankfully, he wasn't too old that he didn't mind reaching up to give her a hug. "It's not so bad. I guess I don't hate school as much as I used to."

Maybe the worst of his grief was fading. She

hoped so, for his sake. "I'm glad." She returned his hug and pressed a kiss to his forehead, wishing she could ease his pain in some way. He was growing up so fast. "Good night, Josh."

"G'night." He yawned and she laughed softly, crossing the room to turn out the light and then closing the door behind her.

It was only nine o'clock, and as she wasn't quite ready to go to bed herself, she wandered down the hall, looking for Austin. He wasn't in the kitchen or in the living room, watching TV. The patio doors in the living room were open, leading to the enclosed backyard, and she found him sitting outside on a lounge chair, wearing a T-shirt and swim trunks, using his toe to make waves in the calm water of his pool.

"Bet you'll have trouble sleeping tonight, huh?" she asked, coming out to stand beside him. "It's hard to get back on a normal schedule when you've pulled an all-night shift."

"Maybe a little," he admitted. He gestured to the empty lounge chair beside him. "Have a seat. I was just thinking of going for a swim. Care to join me?"

A swim with Austin sounded like heaven. The cool water looked as if it would soothe her ragged nerves. Yet at the same time she knew that accepting Austin's offer wouldn't be the smartest thing she'd ever done.

She liked him far too much already. More so after everything he'd done for Josh.

"I don't know." She hesitated, trying to think of a good excuse not to. Difficult to come up with something when she really wanted to join him.

"Please?" He stood, stripped off his T-shirt and jumped into the water, making a huge splash and raining drops of water on her heated skin. Sluicing water off his face, he tossed back his wet hair and grinned. "Swimming alone isn't much fun. Come on in. The water is awesome."

She wavered, torn between what she wanted and what was smart. Thinking back to their kiss in the kitchen, she was mortified to realize he'd

pulled away from her. Because he was only interested in fun? She'd thought at the time he'd
pulled away because she wasn't his type.

But things had changed since then. They were
friends. Surely two friends could hang out
together without getting all weird about it. "All
right. I'll get my swimsuit on."

She thought she heard him mutter, "Don't
bother with a suit on my account," as she walked
away, but figured she must have misheard. Since
that heated kiss they'd shared, he'd been nothing
but polite. Annoyingly so. She hurried inside,
and then dug through her dresser until she found
her swimsuit.

It was a modest emerald green one-piece,
although when she walked back outside, she felt
extremely self-conscious wearing the figure-
hugging nylon. Austin was doing laps length-
wise in the pool so she stood at the edge and
dipped her toe in, testing the water temperature.

Cool, but not unbearably so. Refreshing in the
muggy heat of the night. Before she could lower

herself to the edge a hand grabbed her foot and jerked her off balance.

"Yikes!" she squeaked, before plunging into the cool depths of the pool.

When she emerged she heard Austin's deep chuckle. The sound soothed her ire. She hadn't heard him laugh much lately. "You'd better watch out, buster," she threatened. "I don't get mad, I get even."

"Oh, yeah?" he taunted. "Give it your best shot, babe."

Babe? She wasn't anyone's babe. Betting that Austin didn't know she'd spent several summers on the beach as a lifeguard, she slid beneath the water and silently made her way across the pool. When she found his legs, treading water, she gave a hard yank and then jackknifed out of reach.

They goofed around in the water, each trying to sneak up and dunk the other. Austin was fast, but she had stealth, keeping the score fairly even until Austin caught her off guard for a second dunking moments after the first one.

She pushed off the bottom of the pool, breaking the surface while coughing and sputtering, having swallowed a mouthful of water.

Austin's strong arms lifted her up, holding her safely against his chest while she struggled to breathe.

"I'm sorry. Are you all right?" he asked, his tone contrite.

She gasped between coughs, "I give up. You win." She rested her hands on his slick, broad shoulders to help maintain her balance.

"I'm sorry," he repeated in a low tone. His chest was warm, her legs entangling with his as he held her.

"I'm OK," she managed, although she wasn't certain it was true. Being close to him was wreaking havoc with her common sense. Her breasts were pressed against him, the tips aching with desire, and she knew she'd better move away before she did something she'd regret.

Although she honestly couldn't say she'd experienced regrets after kissing him the other night.

Their bodies bumped together in the buoyant water. His arms tightened, holding her close.

"Lindsey," he murmured, smoothing her wet hair away from her face before lowering his head toward her mouth. She met him halfway, eager to taste him.

Oh, heavens, this kiss was much better than the first. This time there wasn't any hesitation. The moment their mouths touched, she parted her lips, inviting him deeper.

She barely noticed when he drew her toward the shallow end of the pool. When he stumbled on the steps, she broke free.

"Austin?" she wasn't sure what she was asking.

"Come here, to the lounger." Austin's voice was low, rough with need. "We need to talk."

"Talk?" She blinked, trying to read his expression in the darkness. Since when did a guy stop kissing a woman in order to talk?

A low chuckle escaped him and he stretched out on the lounger, pulling her down beside him. There was barely room for both of them.

"Lindsey, I think it's obvious how much I want you. But I promised you could stay here without strings. This isn't a part of our deal."

He was sweet, the way he spoke so earnestly. "I know," she said, not sure what else to say. She honestly didn't believe he expected her to sleep with him as a part of their deal.

"I don't want to give you a reason to leave," he admitted finally.

She wet her dry mouth with her tongue. Never had she wanted a man as much as she wanted Austin. For so long passion had been missing from her life. She found she couldn't walk away from it now. "Maybe I'm looking for a reason to stay."

"I'd like that," he murmured, before capturing her mouth in another deep kiss. This time she could feel the evidence of his arousal as he molded her body to his.

When his fingers brushed the curve of her breast, finding the tight nipple through the thin fabric of her suit, she arched against him, wishing her swimsuit, the one that had seemed so scanty before, would simply disappear.

She trailed her hand down his back, finding the top edge of his waistband. His trunks needed to disappear, too.

"Lindsey, please, be sure about this…" he whispered, as she slid her fingertips beneath the elastic waistband.

"I'm sure." She followed the curve of his butt, marveling at the sculpted muscles. His hands tugged at her swimsuit, trying to free her breasts.

"Mom? My stomach hurts."

They both froze at the sound of Josh's voice. Lindsey scrambled off Austin, trying to pull the straps of her swimsuit back into place.

"Too much pizza," she whispered, running a hand along her body to make sure she was safely back together. "I'm sorry."

"It's OK, I understand," Austin assured her.

Lindsey headed inside to find Josh, ruefully wondering if Austin had ever been interrupted by one of his girlfriend's kids before tonight.

Somehow she doubted it.

What was she thinking, playing with fire? She was lucky that Josh had interrupted when he had, before she managed to get burned.

Josh finally fell asleep, after she'd given him some medication she'd found in Austin's medicine cabinet. By the next morning, Josh was tired but otherwise felt fine and insisted on going to school.

She'd been tempted to keep him at home. Especially as both she and Austin had the day off and she couldn't help reliving those moments at the side of his pool.

Was he planning to pick up where they'd left off?

Did she want him to?

Months ago she'd accused Austin of trying to take over her life. But while that was sort of true, the real reason she'd pushed him away had been because she'd known it would be like this between them. Hot. Sensual. Intense. Far too tempting.

She needed to get a grip. Deciding it was best

if she kept busy, Lindsey drove to the bank to check on the status of her loan.

The loan officer kept her waiting almost twenty minutes. When he finally returned, she could tell by the serious expression on his face that the news wasn't promising.

"I'm sorry, Mrs Winters, but you didn't qualify for a loan."

Stunned, she stared at him. "I need to pay for the repairs on my house. What do you suggest I do?"

He shifted uncomfortably in his chair, tugging at his tie. "There are places that will give high-risk loans to people like you for a much higher interest rate. You might want to try one of them."

Annoyed, she grabbed her purse and stood. "Thanks for nothing," she told him, before walking out of the bank, her cheeks burning with embarrassment. A high-interest loan because she was high risk. The payments were going to be difficult enough, without adding a high-interest rate to the mix.

Depressed, she headed over to her house to check

on the status of the repairs. Inside, she could see evidence of work that had been done, bits of wiring scattered around the floor, along with a fine sheen of drywall dust, but the place was empty.

Where were the workers? Was it a holiday of some sort? Columbus Day? Presidents' Day? She frowned. No holiday that she could remember.

Austin showed up, surprised to find her there. "What's wrong?" he asked when he saw the expression on her face.

"Where is everyone? Why aren't they working?"

"The crew is working on a couple of projects at the same time," he explained. "This is the height of the building season and besides, it's one of the reasons their bid was lower. I knew it was going to take a little longer this way."

"I thought you were going to put a rush on this?" she said abruptly, knowing she sounded angry but unable to help herself.

He frowned. "I tried, Lindsey, but I figured cheaper was better."

She let her breath out in a deep, heavy sigh.

How could she argue with cheaper? Heck, even the cheaper rates were going to be difficult to pay. Especially without her bank loan.

Austin pointed out what the electricians were doing, going into a technical explanation of how they were going to bring the wiring up to code. Then he showed her the water-damaged drywall, extending over half the corner of her house.

It would take weeks to get everything completed. If they were lucky.

She forced herself to meet Austin's gaze. "I was turned down for a bank loan. I'm going to look into other options, but you need to know, I'll figure out some way to pay you back."

"No problem," he quickly assured her. "Don't even worry about paying me back. Just make sure you and Josh have what you need."

A flash of anger burned in her belly. Did he expect her to borrow money from him? Then conveniently forget to pay him back? What sort of person did he think she was? "If it takes longer to get a loan approved, I'll pay the going interest rate, in addition to the balance of the amount you've paid out so far."

He scowled. "Don't be ridiculous. I'm not going to make money from helping you, Lindsey. Forget about paying any interest. I told you, don't worry about the money."

"No. I won't forget about the interest or the money." She crossed her arms over her chest. "I know you sincerely care about my welfare, Austin, but there's no reason to act as if I can't support myself." She'd considered asking him for a loan, but not anymore. The high-interest place would be a much better way to go.

Especially after the heated kisses they'd exchanged beneath the stars last night.

"There is another way to do this," he said in a low tone.

"There is?" Warily she looked at him. "Like what?"

"You could marry me and move in with me permanently."

CHAPTER EIGHT

AUSTIN hadn't planned to propose, but the moment the words had left his mouth he realized marrying Lindsey was the perfect solution.

Too bad that Lindsey's reaction wasn't exactly encouraging.

She went pale, her eyes widened and her pupils dilated to the point he couldn't see the blue of her irises. She shook her head, taking several steps backward as if needing to get away from him.

"Marry you? Are you kidding?" Her voice rose, nearly hysterical. "No. Oh, no. Absolutely not."

He tried not to be hurt by her flat-out refusal. His fault, for blurting out the proposal without any forewarning. And, hell, couldn't he have chosen a more romantic setting? But she didn't have to act as if being with him was totally out of the question. Their relationship had gone from mere friendship to a heck of a lot more on the patio surrounding his pool last night.

If not for Josh's upset stomach, he was fairly sure they would have made love. The memory of having Lindsey in his arms, wearing nothing but a scrap of a swimsuit, was enough to make him hard and aching. He was trying to prove he wasn't interested in a fling or a one-night stand.

He was interested in far more.

"Lindsey, I know I shouldn't have blurted it out like that, but I want you to know I'm serious. I— We don't have to do anything right away. Just think about it, OK?" He took a step toward her.

"No!" she shouted. She spun on her heel and practically ran from the house. He took off after her, but she was surprisingly quick, jumping into her car and backing out of the driveway almost before he could blink. She drove down Puckett Street as if the hounds from hell were hot on her heels.

He stared after her bright yellow car, watching as the taillights disappeared around the corner.

Sighing heavily, he massaged the muscles behind his neck.

Damn. His impatience had caused him to blow it with Lindsey, big time.

Lindsey was so upset her hands were shaking. She couldn't believe Austin had actually proposed to her. Out of pure pity! To help her avoid being in debt!

Worse, she'd almost said yes. Had been far too tempted to say yes.

What was wrong with her? She was sending conflicting signals to Austin, wrestling in the pool with him one minute, arguing over her house repairs the next. No wonder he'd proposed. Was she more like her mother than she'd realized? She needed to move out of Austin's house as soon as possible.

Some of her panic deflated though when she went to a high-interest brokerage house and saw just how much she'd have to pay on a monthly basis. One extra shift a pay period wouldn't be enough. She'd have to work two extra shifts in order to make ends meet.

Still, she didn't want Austin to think she'd marry him to avoid paying her debts, so she signed the papers and walked away with a fat check and high loan payments.

At Austin's house, she set the check in the center of the kitchen table, where Austin couldn't help but see it when he came home.

Austin wasn't her type. She knew his reputation wasn't exaggerated. Many a nurse in the ED had raved over what it had been like to go out with him. His proposal had caught her so off guard, she didn't know what to do or to say.

Avoiding him wasn't easy, with them living in one house. Where could she go if she and Josh did need to move out? She couldn't afford a hotel, not with the loan payments. She had friends from work, but none of them had much extra room. She sat on the edge of the bed in

Austin's spare bedroom and gazed around helplessly.

She was stuck here until she could find another place to stay.

Austin knew how much he'd blown it with Lindsey when she avoided him for the rest of the day. He saw the check on the kitchen table from one of those high-interest loan places, but refused to take it.

Hefty interest payments wouldn't help her become independent. She was already independent, doing a fine job of raising her son on her own. Why couldn't she see that?

He rubbed the back of his neck, trying to relax his tense muscles. He shouldn't have shocked her with his proposal. Although he'd meant every word. The thought of marrying Lindsey didn't scare him as much as it probably should have. He'd never really planned on marrying anyone. The women he'd dated hadn't remotely interested him enough to consider spending the rest of his life with one of them.

And despite his tendency to avoid relationships, he didn't take marriage lightly. Thanks to the example set by his parents, he believed in marrying for keeps. One of the reason's he'd been so picky before.

Giving Lindsey the space she needed wasn't easy. Especially when he missed talking to her.

He was almost grateful he could leave to go to work the next day. Living in the same house with her when she was barely speaking to him wasn't easy.

He got his first call within the hour, responding to a bad single-vehicle crash on the interstate highway. After hitting a concrete barrier, the vehicle had flipped over and skidded on its roof for almost fifty feet.

Austin was glad he was partnered with Big Joe to assist with the extrication. Two teams had been dispatched to the scene of the crash and traffic was backed up for miles. Luckily, both occupants of the car, a husband and his wife, had been wearing their seat belts.

"Are you all right?" he asked, kneeling down to peer into the space where the driver's side window had once been. The driver looked to be worse off than the female passenger.

"My chest hurts."

Austin didn't like the way the guy looked— he was pale, sweaty and complaining of chest pain. Had he suffered a heart attack before the crash or as a result of flipping over the concrete barrier and sliding on the car's roof for fifty feet?

"Let's get some oxygen on him," he said, reaching in to wrap the oxygen mask around the guy's head. "On a scale of one to ten, with ten being the worst pain you've ever felt, how much does your chest hurt?"

"Eight. Maybe a nine." The man's words were muffled by the oxygen mask.

"Let's try some nitroglycerine," Big Joe said, pulling out the small vial of soluble tablets.

He urged the patient to place the medication under his tongue. While they gave the nitro a chance to work, they discussed the best way to get him out of the car.

"Through the window," Big Joe decided. He gave a yank on the door, but it wouldn't budge. "Unless we want to wait for the jaws of life to get here?"

"No, let's try the window. I'll cut through his seat belt." Austin used his knife to free the driver, and then slowly eased him out of the car, doing his best to keep the guy's head and neck in alignment.

"How's the pain?" he asked, when the driver's head was free.

"A little better." The guy lifted bloody hands to his chest, rubbing the center. "Still hurts, though."

"Joe, start an IV to give him some morphine." Austin didn't like the driver's pale, cold, clammy skin. They needed to get his pain under control, and quickly.

With Big Joe's help he managed to get the driver free of the car and safely strapped onto the long board. Using padded head and shoulder blocks, he kept the guy's neck stabilized as Joe started the first IV.

The driver relaxed once they had the IV morphine in him. But hooking him up to the portable monitor showed he had some acute myocardial changes going on in his heart. Austin called the hospital and discussed the case with the ED doctor as they prepared to transport him for further treatment.

A doctor met them at the doorway of the ED, and Austin swallowed the stab of disappointment that Lindsey wasn't there, as well. The transfer of care went very smoothly. The doctor had already contacted the cardiologist on duty and was discussing the need for the patient to go straight to the cardiac catheterization lab.

Austin was glad they'd been able to get the poor guy out of his car without taking too much time.

He saw Lindsey taking care of the passenger of the motor vehicle crash, and as much as he wished he could talk to her, now wasn't the time.

She saw him, though, and acknowledged him with a nod and a smile.

Had she gotten over being mad at him? He knew she wasn't the type to hold a grudge for long. He wished more than anything they had time to talk. Maybe tomorrow, after his twenty-four-hour shift was over, they'd have time.

The rest of his day remained busy. He'd thought about calling Lindsey a least a dozen times, but managed to talk himself out of it. Better to make sure their next conversation was in person.

That night, as he stared up at the ceiling over his bunk in the fire station, he relived those moments at his pool. The fun they'd had playing in the water, and then the kiss that had turned innocence into burning desire.

He was dreaming of Lindsey when the fire bells went off. The alarm had the effect that the moment he heard them he jumped out of bed and slid down the fire pole before he was fully awake. He stepped into his gear and was seated on the truck in less than two minutes, wishing there had been time for coffee to help clear the cobwebs of sleep from his mind.

"Three-alarm blaze in an apartment building on Hickory Avenue," Big Joe informed him.

He nodded, indicating he'd understood in spite of the sirens blaring as they flew through the streets. Apartment building fires were not good—too many potential victims.

The ride to the fire didn't take long as there was little traffic at four-thirty in the morning. Austin jumped out of the truck, taking the point position of going in first.

There were lots of people already huddled outside. The fire chief was already on scene, giving orders. "There's a family of five not accounted for yet in apartment number 318, and an elderly couple in unit number 314 located on either side of the burning unit. We suspect the fire has already spread into the roof. Monroe, you and Joe go in after the family of five—there's a five-year-old boy and a six-year-old girl. The youngest child is just an infant. Hanks and

Bishop, take the elderly couple. I have more responders on the way if you need help. Let's go."

Austin didn't need to be told twice. The thought of kids being trapped in the apartment was horrifying. He took a second to be thankful Lindsey and Josh were safe before he took the stairs up to the third-floor apartment.

Smoke thicker than pea soup hung in the hallway when he reached the top. Keeping his breathing even through the face mask, Austin made his way down the hall to the apartment housing the family of five. He tested the door with his gloved hand, gauging the wood for warmth before kicking the door in.

The smoke was even more dense inside. Had the fire from the neighboring apartment come through into this unit? The source of the fire was reported to be someplace in the kitchen. It was possible the kitchens of each apartment butted up against each other.

He glanced around but didn't see any sign of life, so he headed down the hall to the bedrooms.

They found the kids' bedroom first, but he only saw one child in bed, the girl. The other bed was empty. He motioned for Big Joe to go in for the six-year-old girl while he continued making his way down to the second bedroom. The parents were there, with a small infant in a cradle at the foot of the bed.

He was amazed they were all sleeping in spite of the thick smoke. Obviously, if they had smoke alarms, they weren't working. He picked up the baby and then woke up the parents.

The couple moved slowly, as if they were drugged. Which in a way they were as the smoke had robbed their brains of oxygen. He carried the infant outside, using his radio to let the ground crew know they'd found the survivors.

He and Big Joe handed the kids over to the paramedic crew and then hurried back inside for the parents. And where was the third child? The parents couldn't even walk under their own power, so he and Big Joe carried them down the stairs to the fresh air outside.

"We lost the roof. I need every firefighter to get the hell out of the building—now!" his fire chief shouted.

"We're missing a child," Austin told him. "I'm going back in."

His boss glanced up at the building where flames could be seen shooting from the roof. "No. It's too dangerous."

"I'll be quick. He's only five years old." Austin ran back inside before his boss could order him to stand down. He knew the other child was in there somewhere. Hiding under the bed? Or maybe in the bathroom? He didn't know for sure, but he wouldn't rest until he'd found him.

He checked the bathroom first, but it was empty. Searching the kids' bedroom next, he crawled on the floor, peering under the bed. Sure enough, he saw the shape of a small child curled up in the corner furthest from the edge of the bed.

"Come on, buddy, it's OK. We need to go outside." He reached his arm under the bed, groping for the boy. When he touched the boy, the kid screamed.

He snatched his arm back. What the hell? Was the boy hurt? He didn't want to make things worse, so he stood up, grabbed the headboard of the bed and tipped the entire frame up on its end, so he could see the child.

The kid was coughing and crying hysterically, but there were no other signs of injury. Lifting his face mask off, he placed it on the young boy for a few moment. He knew it was better to keep his own mask on, but the way the kid was coughing and crying, the boy needed oxygen more than he did at the moment.

"Come on, buddy, we need to get out of here." He put his face mask back on, picked the child up and made his way back to the hallway. When he reached the living room, a loud crack echoed through the room and parts of the ceiling came crashing down on his head.

Pressing the child's head to his chest, he hunched his shoulders, protecting the boy as best he could as he made his way to the door. The entire apartment was on fire now, and he knew they didn't have much time. Something from the ceiling hit him in the back and he stumbled to his knees, barely hanging onto the boy with one arm as he used the other to brace himself from falling on his face.

Just when Austin was beginning to fear he wouldn't make it out of the apartment after all, Big Joe loomed in the doorway. "Monroe?"

"Here." Giving a last gigantic push, he stood and stumbled toward his partner. For a moment Sam's face swam before him. He blinked and saw Big Joe, who hauled him toward the stairwell.

"Your back is smoking. What happened?" Big Joe asked, as they stepped over debris on the floor.

He couldn't answer, but followed Big Joe's lead down the stairs and outside. He was surprised to discover the sun was already up. Somehow he must have been inside the building longer than he'd thought.

The paramedic crew surrounded him, taking

the boy from his arms and then pulling off his gear. He tried to tell them he was fine, but his voice came out as a weak croak.

They slapped oxygen on his face and hustled him over to the waiting ambulance. The continued plucking at his clothes and he yelped in pain when they found the spot in the center of his back that burnt like the devil.

One of them slapped a cold towel over the spot, which helped a little. "Get him to the hospital, stat."

"I'm fine," he managed, his voice still husky. But he was too weak to push them away when they bundled him onto the stretcher.

How odd to be the patient when he was normally on the other side of the bed. Visions of the wildfire he'd fought alongside Sam danced at the edge of his mind. He must have blacked out for a few minutes because suddenly he was in the brightly lit ED with faces leaning over him.

Lindsey's face? His gaze clung to the familiar features as he tried to reassure her he was fine.

The frank concern in her eyes and the seriousness of her expression betrayed the depth of her worry.

As they gave him some medication to help with the pain, his last conscious thought was regret that he'd put that expression in her eyes. He wasn't only responsible for himself.

He was responsible for Lindsey and Josh, as well. He needed to take better care of himself, for their sakes.

Lindsey couldn't believe it when the ambulance crew wheeled in Austin as her first patient of the day. The ED was swamped with other victims from the fire, too.

Austin saved a young boy's life.

Almost at the expense of his own.

As she helped to care for Austin, she was relieved to note his injuries weren't life threatening. His lungs didn't sound the greatest, and the ED physician ordered him to stay on thirty percent oxygen via face mask until his pulse ox readings crept up to the ninety percent range.

"Lindsey?"

She heard her name and hurried over to see Austin had finally woken up. The morphine dose they'd given him had put him under for almost thirty minutes. Thank heavens, his vital signs remained stable. "I'm here." She took his hand in hers, giving him a reassuring squeeze. "How are you feeling?"

"Better." His voice was husky, and would have been sexy if she hadn't been worried about his vocal cords swelling from the smoke damage. "Water?"

"Sure." She helped him to sit up and held the cup for him as he drank from a plastic cup. Seeing Austin helpless shook her more than she cared to admit. "The boy? Do you know how the young boy is doing?"

She knew he meant Noah Pickerson, the boy who'd been taken by helicopter to the Children's Hospital in LA. "They flew him to Children's for closer observation."

A frown furrowed his brow. "Children's?"

"Yes. His breathing wasn't so good. They were talking about possibly using hyperbaric treatments on him, which we don't have here."

Austin frowned. "He was in the apartment too long. We couldn't find him. He was hiding under the bed."

She put a soothing hand on his forearm. "It's not your fault, Austin. You saved his life by finding him when you did."

His crooked smile was sheepish. "Guess I'm not used to being the patient."

"No kidding," she responded in a dry tone. Austin was always so strong, invincible. He'd been lucky his injuries weren't worse.

"I'm sorry," he whispered, his eyes half-closed with fatigue. "I shouldn't have proposed… Stupid…"

She stared at him, holding her breath. Stupid for wanting to marry her? She frowned, not liking that idea. Although maybe he realized marrying her to keep her out of debt was stupid, and on that she'd have to agree.

She wasn't so broke that she needed to accept Austin's pity proposal. She'd be fine. She'd make the high monthly payments by working an extra shift each week. She'd make it.

She had no choice but to make it.

They kept Austin for observation for several hours. The burnt area of his back wasn't too bad, although the area would need dressing changes daily with Silvadene cream.

When the ED physician finally released him, she realized he didn't have a way to get home.

"I'll give you a ride," she offered.

"Thanks." His voice was still a little hoarse but she thought it sounded a much better than before.

At the last minute she remembered the need to pick up Josh from his Tai Kwon Do class. Good grief, what sort of mother forgot about her own son?

When she went to get Josh a little later, she told him about Austin. "He was hurt during a fire, but he's fine."

"He was hurt?" Josh's eyes widened in alarm. "What happened? Did he get burnt?"

"No, he's not burnt," she hastened to assure him, skating over the truth. Too late, she remembered Josh had lost his father to a fire. "He's fine, Josh, I promise."

Josh dashed outside to see for himself.

Lindsey followed more slowly. She was grateful for Austin's influence on Josh, but it was clear her son had grown too attached to Austin.

She needed to move back to her own house as soon as possible, to protect him from being hurt worse in the long run.

CHAPTER NINE

LINDSEY threw together a quick, early dinner, and then sat down to help Josh with his homework, fighting an insane need to check on Austin every three minutes.

Josh wasn't the only one who'd grown dependent on him. She'd gotten used to having Austin around, as well. Despite her cheerful façade for Josh's benefit, she'd been worried about him, too.

"Can I go and talk to Austin now?" Josh asked the minute he'd finished his math homework. His fourth-grade math homework that was almost over her head. What was she going to do when he reached high school? She dreaded thinking about it.

"Don't wake him up if he's sleeping," she cautioned. "He was up most of the night, working."

She wasn't surprised when Josh returned a few minutes later, his tiny shoulders slumped with disappointment. "He is sleeping, Mom. Are you sure he's OK? He's gonna wake up, right?"

"Oh, Josh, of course he's going to wake up." Aching for her son's obvious distress, she gave him a quick hug. "Stop worrying, OK? You know he works twenty-four hours straight. He's just tired, that's all."

"I guess." Josh didn't look convinced. "Maybe I shouldn't go to Tony's house this weekend."

Now she knew Josh was seriously worried. Usually there wasn't anything that would have caused him to consider giving up going to his friend's birthday party sleepover. At first she hadn't really wanted Josh to go because, selfishly, she didn't want to be home alone with Austin. But after Austin's brush with death, she figured Josh could use a little distance and she had been glad he'd been planning to go. "Why don't you talk to Austin about it later?" she suggested, knowing Austin would encourage him to go and have fun. "Then decide what to do."

Her ruse worked. Austin woke up a few hours later and she asked Josh to carry in his dinner, giving them a chance to talk.

"He said I should go to Tony's house," Josh said, returning with the empty dishes a while later. "He's really fine, Mom."

Refraining from stating the obvious—*I told you so*—she nodded. "Good. Get your things together, so that we can take them to school with you tomorrow." The boys were going straight to Tony's house after school on Friday, and staying through until Sunday.

Two full days without any parental responsibilities.

Two full days alone with Austin.

Well, not exactly two full days because as soon as Josh had been invited to the party, she'd signed up to work some additional weekend shifts, knowing she should take advantage of the chance to work extra hours without needing to arrange for a babysitter.

Sixteen hours of work didn't seem like much time to keep them apart, though.

Especially when she knew she'd have to help him with the dressing changes on the burnt area in the center of his back.

Lindsey had forgotten how busy Friday nights were in the ED. Since going back to work, after Josh had started school, she'd mostly picked up day shifts or the occasional weekend if Sam was going to be home.

But Friday nights were crazier than any other night of the week.

At least keeping busy made the night go faster.

She started to wonder if it was a full moon when the police brought in several psych patients. Her admission was some guy who'd stripped down to his bare butt while standing in the middle of the street, talking to himself. When they'd asked him to put his pants back on, he'd begun to swear loudly, arguing with them and generally acting crazy. Assuming he needed medication of some sort, they'd brought him in to be evaluated.

Thankfully, they'd gotten him to put his pants back on first.

The police officer who'd brought in the psych patient was Officer MacDonald. Shaun MacDonald was a nice quiet guy who happened to be a single parent, too.

"Hey, Lindsey, how are you?" he asked.

"Pretty good. How about you? How's your daughter?"

"Better." His daughter, Morgan, was older than Josh, in her early teens. Shaun had talked about her on more than one occasion.

"I'm glad." She blew her bangs off her forehead. "Is it a full moon out there or what? Could you guys stop bringing in psych patients, please?"

"Do you think we're having fun?" Shaun joked. "Like I want to see some guy with his pants off?"

That made her laugh.

"Ah, Lindsey, are you doing anything next weekend? I'm off work and thought maybe we could go out for dinner or something."

"What?" She stared at Shaun, completely taken aback by his invitation. No one had asked her out since Sam's death. She and Shaun had always been friends, he'd never hinted at wanting more. She wasn't sure who was crazier, the guy who'd taken off his pants in the middle of the street or Shaun MacDonald. "Thanks, but I don't think so."

"I understand," Shaun said quickly, his face turning bright red. "I just thought, seeing as we're both single parents, that maybe, ah, hell. Never mind."

"It was sweet of you to ask," she said quickly, not wanting him to feel bad. "I'm sorry, but I'm just not ready."

"It's OK. Although if that changes, give me a call." He handed her a card with his name and number on it.

Bemused, she took Shaun's card, watching as

he walked away. Shaun MacDonald was a nice-looking guy, but she wasn't remotely interested in going out with him. Or anyone.

The thought of kissing any man that wasn't Austin left a sour taste in her mouth.

She closed her eyes and rubbed her temple. How had this happened? How had she managed to get hung up on the one guy who was totally wrong for her?

Shaun MacDonald was a single parent, just like her. He'd been married before and knew what he was getting into. He had to know something about marriage and relationships.

Austin was a guy who'd played the field, never settling down in a serious relationship. He had no idea what it was like to be a husband or a father.

So why couldn't she find a way to get him out of her system?

Lindsey was exhausted by the time she returned to Austin's house just before midnight, but that didn't stop her from checking on him.

He was still awake, glancing up at her when she walked in. "How was your shift?" he asked in his deep, raspy voice.

"Wicked." She was happy to see he seemed back to normal. "There's a full moon so the crazies were out."

He grimaced in sympathy. "Bummer."

"Are you ready for your dressing change?" she asked, glancing at the stack of sterile dressings on his dresser.

"Sure." He didn't move right away, though, but continued to look at her. "I really appreciate your help with this. If I could reach behind to do these dressing changes myself, I would."

"I know." And she did understand. Still, after the way he'd rescued her after the fire and brought her here to live with him, she was glad the shoe was on the other foot for once. It felt good to be the one helping him. "Turn over, so I can reach your back."

He quirked a brow but did as she asked, flipping over onto his stomach and scrunching up the pillow beneath his chest. The muscles rippled in his arms and she had to swallow hard and avert her gaze to return to the reason she was here.

His wound. Dressing changes.

Wiping her hands on her scrub pants, she gingerly sat on the edge of his bed. "Peeling tape off," she warned as she gently stripped the old dressing off his back. She didn't have a vast experience with burns, but they oozed a lot and the thick dressing was soaked.

He didn't make a sound but she could tell his muscles were tense as he braced himself. He was lucky the burn wasn't worse—the pink area looked relatively healthy, without any sign of infection.

"Looks good," she told him.

She stood and went into his adjoining bathroom to wash her hands and fetch a washcloth, soap and water. After cleaning the area, she patted it dry and then drew on gloves to apply the Silvadene cream.

Throughout the entire procedure, Austin didn't say anything. She wasn't sure if it was because the dressing changes hurt worse than he let on, or if he just couldn't think of anything to chat about.

She'd just finished taping the new dressing over the cream when he let out a low groan.

"What's wrong?" She saw his right shoulder was quivering and she put her hand on his heated skin. "Muscle spasm?"

"Yeah," he said in a low voice. "It'll go away soon."

She wasn't sure she believed him, the way the muscles looked to be jumping out of his skin. She stripped off her gloves, quickly went into the bathroom to wash her hands, then came back to sit beside him. No way could she just sit there and watch as he writhed in pain.

All nurses were taught some simple massage techniques. She wasn't an expert by any means, but she figured anything was better than doing nothing. When she began to knead the sore muscles he groaned again, but this time she could tell it was a murmur of appreciation.

Trying to massage his neck and shoulders was awkward while sitting on the side of his bed. Her own back muscles were straining in protest so she got up and climbed on the bed, bracing her knees on either side of his waist. The position was a little embarrassing, but she decided to maintain a professional attitude.

She was helping to relieve his muscle spasm, nothing sexual about that.

Of course, she would have had to be dead not to notice his muscles. The breadth of his shoulders. The firm flesh of his biceps and the musky scent of his skin. The way his lean body tapered to his narrow waist. She smoothed her hands over his skin, marveling at the differences in a man's body.

As he relaxed, her kneading strokes became longer, smoothing over his muscles with less pressure than she'd applied before.

"Lindsey," he croaked, in his raspy voice. "You're killing me. Don't stop."

She had to laugh at the way he'd contradicted

himself. Yet his muscles did seem to be better, not nearly as knotted as when she'd started.

Maybe she should stop.

She didn't want to stop.

Full of regret, she pulled her hands from his skin and tried to climb off him. But somehow he turned and caught her, dragging her down beside him.

Her heart hammered in her chest as she gazed up at him, his green eyes glittering with need. He didn't say anything, but simply covered her mouth with his.

His kiss overwhelmed her, filling her with edgy desire that rippled all the way down to her toes. His chest was bare, the dusting of hair springy beneath her fingertips. Throwing caution aside, she wrapped her arms around his neck and dragged him closer.

He wedged her legs apart with his knee, before settling himself firmly between her legs. Cupping her face in his hands, he kissed her again, gently this time, as if he was trying to keep himself under control.

She didn't want him to be controlled. She wanted him to lose it. She wanted to feel wild, wanton and wonderful. She kissed him back, urgently.

He tore his mouth from hers, breathing deep. "Lindsey, are you sure about this?" He rested his forehead against hers. "Please. I need you to be sure."

"Yes." She smiled, very much liking the fact he was just as affected by their kisses as she was. "I'm sure."

She thought he whispered something like, "Thank You, God," before he kissed her again, even as he began to peel off her scrubs. It wasn't an easy task with their legs entangled, but as she felt just as overdressed, she helped by arching her back so he could rip the top off over her head.

The laces at her waist were easily dispatched and soon there was nothing between them but his boxers. She slid her hands beneath the waistband, seeking the tight gluteal muscles beneath.

Good heavens, every muscle on Austin's body was awesome.

"Wait." He lifted his head, glancing around with a dazed expression. "Need a condom."

As much as she didn't like the interruption, she was grateful he'd thought of protection as she hadn't. What was wrong with her? Hadn't she learned her lesson with Sam? She loved Josh with her whole heart, but one unplanned pregnancy was bad enough. Repeating the mistake would be just plain stupid.

Austin leaned over to his bedside table, rummaged in the drawer and came up with a small foil packet, his eyes gleaming with triumph.

Then the brief interruption was over as he quickly took care of the condom and then kissed her again, making her head spin even as he urged her to wrap her legs around his waist so he could thrust deep.

He murmured endearments between kisses. He was firm yet gentle at the same time, worshiping her with his body until she thought she'd die from the pleasure. Never had a man put so much effort into lovemaking. He explored every inch of her body, with his hands and then with his mouth.

One orgasm wasn't enough, he pushed for more. Until she felt as if she were being catapulted over the edge of a cliff.

She hadn't given a thought to the wound on his back until he rolled to his side, bringing her with him so they were still nestled together. With her face pressed against his neck, she couldn't speak.

Could barely think.

Austin's breathing slowed, becoming deep, and she might have been irritated to know he'd fallen asleep, except she decided to cut him some slack, knowing he'd been injured.

She breathed in his musky scent, forced to admit the sensual experience she'd just shared with Austin had been unlike anything she'd felt before. Was this why Austin typically only dated girls once before moving on? Because he poured so much of himself into that single night of ecstasy, there wasn't anything left for a second date?

If so, it was no wonder none of the women had voiced a complaint. She certainly wouldn't have, except for one tiny problem.

She was falling in love with him.

Maybe it was the effect of the full moon. Sam had died only a few months ago. She couldn't possibly be falling in love with Austin so soon.

She couldn't trust her feelings, not about something this serious. Her mother always claimed to be in love with the new guy she leapt into a relationship with, too, but, then, in a year or two, their relationship would end and she'd have moved on to the next guy.

Hadn't a similar thing happened with Sam? Not after just a year or two, but it hadn't been long before her marriage had started to unravel.

Squeezing her eyes shut, she tried to block out the memories. There was no way she wanted to fall into the same trap as her mother. Lust was not love.

She refused to expose Josh to her failures.

* * *

Austin woke up when Lindsey tried to sneak out of bed. He reached out to grasp her arm, trying to tug her back under the covers.

"I have to go to the bathroom," she whispered, pulling out of his grasp, so he reluctantly let her go.

She wrapped the sheet around her naked body, but his memory was pretty good. He could remember every detail of their night together without much difficulty.

Making love with Lindsey had been a mind-blowing experience. Well beyond his wildest dreams. Despite his various aches and pains, he wouldn't have minded repeating the performance.

Over and over again.

Unlike his previous relationships, he didn't itch to leave after spending the night together. In fact, he'd already broken his rule with Lindsey. Normally he didn't bring women to his house, preferring going to their place so he could leave whenever he was ready.

Which was usually before the uncomfortable morning-after awkwardness.

Lindsey was different. Last night had definitely been special.

He felt himself grinning like a fool.

Thank heavens for overnight birthday parties. Josh wasn't due home for another twenty-four hours.

They had plenty of time.

Lindsey didn't come back to bed, so after about fifteen minutes he dragged himself up to seek her out.

Was she having morning-after regrets? He scowled. No, she'd been with him all the way. He'd made sure of it.

But then again, there was no telling exactly how convoluted a woman's mind could be.

He found her in the kitchen, fully dressed and rummaging around in his cupboards. Not a good sign.

"Are you hungry?"

"Yes." She wouldn't look at him, and he sensed

she was embarrassed. He crossed the room and took the small frying pan from her hand.

"Sit down. I'll make breakfast." He tried to capture her gaze, to put her at ease.

"No, you're injured. I'll cook."

He hadn't been too injured to make love to her, but refrained from pointing it out. "Lindsey, please. Tell me what's wrong."

"Nothing." She sighed, but reluctantly met his gaze. "I'm just no good at this."

This? Meaning the morning after? He didn't want her to be uncomfortable. "I'm not used to this, either. I don't invite women to my house, ever."

"Ever?" she echoed doubtfully.

He nodded and took a few minutes to pour himself a cup of coffee from the full pot, refilling hers in the process.

She frowned but thanked him.

"Come on, sit down." He sipped his coffee, and then drew her to the kitchen table. "Are you upset with me? About last night?"

"No." She stared at her coffee for a long

moment. "I don't regret last night, but I think it's better if I move back home."

Huh? They'd spent the most incredible night together but she wanted to move back home? Leave? Why?

He was searching for something to say when his phone rang. Lindsey's startled gaze met his. Josh? Who else would call so early on a Saturday morning?

He grabbed the phone. "Hello?"

"Austin?" His younger sister Abby's voice was strained, there was no sign of her usual cheerful self. "Dad had a heart attack. He's on his way to the operating room for emergency open-heart surgery."

CHAPTER TEN

"WHAT happened?" Austin gripped his phone so tightly he was surprised he didn't crush the handset. Details. He wanted details. His father had always been so hale and hearty. His mother was the one who'd been hospitalized after a broken hip a few years ago and had since come down with arthritis. His father had been proud of being in good shape. He'd always gone in for regular physical checkups. How could Abe Monroe be on his way to the operating room for bypass surgery?

"He had chest pain and, at first, the doctor thought they could just place a stent to open his coronary artery, but after they found three different blockages, they decided he needed to go straight to the operating room."

Good grief. He wasn't a doctor but even he knew emergency surgery meant his father's condition was serious. Sounded like he would need a triple bypass to stabilize his heart. Without hesitation he said, "I'll be there as soon as I can arrange a flight to Milwaukee."

"Good. We're at Trinity Medical Center," Abby informed him. "We'll be here in the OR waiting room until we hear from the doctor. Make sure your cell phone is on. We'll call once we know something."

"I will. Thanks for calling, Abby." He hung up the phone to find Lindsey watching him closely.

"Someone's sick?" she guessed, a sympathetic frown furrowing her brow.

"My dad." Austin's own chest was starting to feel tight. Sympathy pains, maybe? His sister Abby was a nurse. Heck, most of his family was in the medical profession in some way. Except for his brother Alec, who was a cop. At least Alec had had the good sense to marry a doctor and, heaven knew, Jillian had plenty of physician connections at Trinity Medical Center.

His dad was in good hands.

Suddenly he missed his family very badly.

"Austin?" Lindsey came forward and placed a reassuring hand on his arm. "What's wrong with your dad?"

He glanced at Lindsey, realizing he'd never really discussed his family with her. Not for any particular reason, just because the subject had never come up. He swallowed hard. "My sister Abby said he's had a heart attack. They tried to place a stent but it didn't work so he's on his way for open-heart surgery. I need to go home."

"To Milwaukee?"

"Yeah." He was surprised Lindsey knew where he lived. He pulled himself together and focused on her compassionate gaze. "Will you come with me?"

"Me?" Her voice squeaked in surprise.

"Yes, you. And Josh, too." He didn't want to analyze his feelings too closely, but he knew he wanted Lindsey there. At his side. He couldn't imagine facing this alone.

In case his dad didn't make it through surgery.

"Why?" she asked, before she could stop herself. From the moment she'd crawled from his bed she'd been embarrassed at how she'd practically thrown herself at Austin with total recklessness. Especially when Sam had never made her feel the same way.

She'd worried all over again that she was just like her mother.

But right now her confused feelings weren't important. Austin's father was very sick. He obviously needed a friend.

"Please? I need your support, Lindsey." His eyes darkened. "In case my dad doesn't make it."

"He will," she said with confidence she didn't feel. She couldn't deny how glad she was that he wanted her near him in this time of crisis. "Of course I'll come."

She hesitated, debating about Josh. If she called Tony's mother, she was pretty sure Becky would agree to keep Josh while they were gone. On the other hand, she had no idea how long they'd need to stay in Milwaukee—much of that depended on how well Austin's father did after surgery. As the next week was a short week in school, the kids were off on Thursday and Friday for teacher inservice days. Josh wouldn't miss much if she pulled him from class.

"We'll both come with you," she decided. Josh would be upset if they kept him out of what was happening. He'd want to be there for Austin, too. "I'll call Tony's mother, to let her know we'll pick him up early."

"I'll make the plane reservations." Austin's expression was dazed, as if the reality hadn't quite hit him yet. He disappeared into his den to book the flight on the computer while she grabbed the phone.

After explaining everything to Becky, she then talked to Josh. He was great, didn't whine a bit about missing the rest of Tony's party, more than willing to go to Milwaukee.

Then she had to call work to arrange to be off. Not an easy feat—it would be a Saturday night shift after all. She had to make several phone calls to attempt to cover her shift. Luckily, one of the other ED nurses she had done a favor for a few months ago came through and agreed to work in her place.

Five hours later, they were at the airport, waiting to board their flight.

Josh's fascination with the process, his first time ever flying in a plane, was enough to keep them from worrying about what was going on in Milwaukee. But once they were seated on the plane, Austin reached across and took her hand in his.

She stared at their entwined fingers for a long moment. She was seated between Austin and Josh, giving her son the window seat so he could enjoy the thrill of flying, and even with Josh sitting right there, able to see how they held hands, she couldn't make herself let go. Clearly Austin was shaken by his father's sudden illness. She couldn't deny him this small bit of support.

She tried to think of a safe topic to discuss. "You mentioned a younger sister, Abby. Do you have other brothers and sisters, as well?"

A faint smile tugged the corner of his mouth. "Yeah. There's a few of us." He was quiet for a moment before glancing at her. "Are you sure you want to hear all this?"

She nodded. Why not? They had plenty of time.

"Abby is the baby of the family, two years younger than I am, and is married to a physical rehab physician named Nick Tremayne. Alec is a cop, he's a year older than I am, and he's married to Jillian, an ED doctor at Trinity Medical Center. That's where my dad is, by the way. Then there's Adam, he's a couple years older than Alec and works as a pediatrician in his own practice. He recently got engaged to Krista Vaughn, one of the pediatric nurses at Children's Memorial."

"Wow," she murmured, when he paused for a breath. "How am I ever going to keep them straight?"

"Don't even try. My parents used all names starting with the letter *A,* which only adds to the confusion. Where did I leave off?" He frowned. "Oh, yeah, Adam. After Adam there's Alaina. She's married to a guy named Scott and has two kids, Bethany and Ben. Oh, I forgot to mention, Alec has a daughter, too, Shelby, who's the same age as Bethany. They're younger than Josh," he added, glancing over at Josh, whose face was plastered against the window. "Just seven years old, but they're good kids. At least he'll have someone to hang out with."

"That's good." The names of Austin's family were buzzing around in her head, making her feel dizzy. She mentally counted backward. "So there are five of you?"

"Six. My oldest brother is Aaron. He's a big-time surgeon at Johns Hopkins Institute. We don't see him much. He was married, but he and

Morganne divorced two years ago. They didn't have any children."

From what he'd described, Aaron's divorce was the oddity in a family who seemed to be all happily married. Except for Austin himself, that was. Hearing about his family now, she wondered why he'd been satisfied with having a string of girlfriends, none of them serious. Had something happened in the past to make him relationship shy? She wished she were bold enough to ask. "Your family sounds wonderful."

"Yeah. They are." Austin's expression was solemn. "Our family is a testament to my parents. We were very lucky, we had a great life growing up. My parents loved us, yet it was even more obvious the way they cared about each other. My dad was pretty freaked out when my mom fell down the stairs and broke her hip a few years ago. I can't imagine what she's going through right now."

The way he spoke about his parents, and the love they had for each other, brought a lump in her throat. He was close to his family, much closer than she would have believed, considering the thousands of miles between Sun Valley, California, and Milwaukee, Wisconsin.

The lump in her throat swelled. If something happened to his dad, would Austin want to stay? Was it possible he'd consider moving back home for good?

They arrived in Milwaukee late, almost eight o'clock at night, partially because of the two-hour time difference between Pacific time and central standard time. As Austin took care of renting a car, she tried to explain the whole time-zone thing to Josh.

"Back home it's still only six o'clock?" he asked, a puzzled frown in his brow. "I don't get it. How can it be one time here and another time someplace else?"

She launched into a discussion about time and the way it continually changed around the world, and the more she talked the more she struggled to explain. Thankfully Austin showed up before she could confuse herself. "Just trust me, the time is different all around the world. In the US it's only a few hours, but in Tokyo or Australia it's half a day. While it's light here, it's dark in Australia and vice versa."

Josh mulled this over as they threw their carry-on luggage in the back of the rental car.

Austin drove straight to the hospital, where he quickly found his family in the family center, the common meeting place for people waiting to hear about loved ones coming out of surgery and those waiting to see those patients in the ICU.

"Austin." Abby ran over to give him a hug. "Dad made it through surgery. Did you get my message?"

"Yeah, I listened to it after we landed. Thanks for the call." He took Lindsey's arm, even though she tried to hang back, giving him space. "This is Lindsey Winters and her son, Josh. Lindsey, this is my family."

The Monroe family took up most of the

waiting area. She glanced over the sea of faces and easily picked out the Monroe brothers from the crowd because of their striking resemblance to Austin. "Hi."

"Welcome, Lindsey." An older woman approached, her expression drawn but a friendly smile on her face nonetheless. "I'm Alice Monroe, Austin's mother. It's wonderful to meet you. I just wish it could be under different circumstances."

"I'm sorry to hear about your husband," Lindsey murmured, feeling awkward, as if she didn't belong here with these people in their time of grief.

"Well, he's gotten through surgery, so I'm hopeful he'll pull through just fine." Alice sounded confident. The rest of the family nodded in agreement.

"Can I go up and see him?" Austin asked.

"Sure. Alaina and Scott are up there now. We've been taking turns," Abby explained. "I'll talk to the nurse and ask her to send Alaina and Scott down so you can go up."

Josh was uncharacteristically shy, standing close

to her side. There were two girls sitting next to each other and a young boy who looked to be about four or five playing a video game on the setup located in the corner of the waiting room. "Why don't you see if you can join Ben's video game?" Lindsay asked, giving him a gentle nudge.

"Will you come up to the ICU with me?" Austin asked in a low voice, when Abby had got off the phone to the nurse. "I might need you to explain a few things."

She wasn't an ICU nurse, but she nodded anyway. Josh went over to join Ben's game, leaving her to follow Austin up to the third-floor surgical ICU.

Austin held her hand the whole elevator ride up. He tensed as they found the ICU and walked in through the main doorway. His dad was located right next to the nurses' station.

She heard Austin take a swift breath, and she didn't blame him for his reaction. Abe was hooked up to a ventilator and numerous IV pumps. Heart rate, blood pressure and pulmonary artery pressures were all displayed on the monitor over his bed. His dad's eyes were closed and she felt Austin hesitate, as if he didn't want to go into the room.

A cute blonde nurse hurried over. "Hi, my name is Tiffany and I'm Mr Monroe's nurse for this evening." Her gaze zeroed in on Austin. "You're one of his sons?"

He nodded, his gaze never wavering from his dad's prone figure. "How is he?"

"Doing really well. We're weaning him off the Nipride, his blood pressure has been coming down nicely and we're also slowly weaning him off the ventilator. Honestly, I know there's lots of equipment in the room, but he's doing fine."

Austin finally turned toward the nurse. "Can he hear us?"

"He's been sleeping a fair amount, from the effects of the pain medicine and the anesthesia. But if you call his name, he'll open his eyes."

Lindsey urged Austin closer. "Come on, take his hand and talk to him, so he knows you're here."

He hung back, resisting. "I don't want to bother him if he's sleeping."

"Most patients rarely remember much of this first night in the ICU," Tiffany explained. "Go ahead. It won't bother him. I've noticed he's calmer when his family is around."

She'd said exactly the right thing to make Austin step closer to the bed, gingerly taking his dad's hand in his. "Hi, Dad. It's me, Austin. Can you hear me?"

Abe opened his eyes, and slowly turned his head to see his son. As their gazes connected, Abe nodded.

"I know you can't talk with that breathing tube in, but I want you to know I'm here and I love you." Austin's voice was low and thick, as he was trying hard to keep it together.

Her eyes pricked with tears as Abe nodded again, trying to smile around the breathing tube in his mouth. Her heart squeezed even tighter when Abe clutched his son's hand as if he wouldn't ever let it go.

* * *

The next day, Lindsey found herself back in the family center, seated among the rest of the Monroe family.

Everyone was so nice, trying to put her at ease and including her in the conversation. She was just starting to remember some of the names and linking them to faces, which, considering the size of Austin's family, was no easy feat.

She was seated beside Austin when his brother Adam, the pediatrician, strolled over.

"Hey, Austin. I see you've finally got a girl of your own, huh?" Adam's eyes swept over her with a frankly admiring glance. "I like her. She's pretty."

She braced herself, waiting to see if Austin would correct his brother's erroneous assumption, but he didn't. "Thanks. I like her, too."

Unsure of what to say, she simply smiled weakly and held her tongue. Austin had asked her to come with him for support because, like a typical health-care professional, he'd expected the worst. But his dad was doing much better now. They'd already gotten word that they'd taken out his breathing tube first thing that morning.

There was no point in reading more into Austin's motives in asking her to come along. And it was possible he just didn't want to go into detail about their convoluted relationship. She couldn't really blame him.

Especially because she wasn't sure they really had a relationship.

She'd enjoyed every minute of their night together. Never had she been loved so thoroughly by a man. He'd made her feel special, as if she were the only woman in his life.

Had he made all the other women feel the same way? She couldn't help but think so. The idea made her wince. It was no doubt a part of his charm.

Austin was an expert at short-term relationships. She had to remember that spending the night with a woman didn't necessarily mean anything.

Yet being included in the Monroe family, as if she were actually a part of the family, gave her a strange sense of belonging. Growing up as an only child, being dragged from one of her mother's relationships to another, had made her feel isolated. She'd never experienced the warm, loving support or the overwhelming teasing of the Monroe family.

She wished she really did belong here.

"Austin, come here for a minute," his brother Alec called.

"Sure." Austin flashed her an apologetic glance, but stood and crossed over to where the brothers were having a quiet discussion. The moment his seat was vacant, Abby slipped into it.

"So, Lindsey, how long have you been seeing my brother?" she asked bluntly.

"Ah…" She glanced helplessly at Austin but he was already deep in conversation and not paying her any attention. "Not long."

"Oh." Abby's crestfallen face betrayed her disappointment. "We were all hoping you were different."

"Different?" Lindsey echoed, not sure exactly what Abby meant.

"Yeah, different." Abby gave a philosophical shrug. "All of Austin's relationships are short-term. We were hoping the reason he brought you along was that your relationship with him was something that might actually last."

CHAPTER ELEVEN

AUSTIN glanced over at Lindsey, catching a glimpse of the alarm in her eyes as Abby talked to her.

Damn. What was Abby saying about him? No doubt, nothing good. He left Alec and Adam to discuss how they were going to support their mother while their dad was in the hospital and went back over to rescue Lindsey.

"Hey, are you ready to go up and visit my dad?" he asked, interrupting whatever Abby was saying.

"Sure." The way Lindsey jumped to her feet convinced him she was eager to leave. Sending his younger sister a warning look, he took Lindsey's hand and walked out of the family center, down the hall toward the elevators.

"Did Abby say something to upset you?" he asked, as they rode up to the third floor.

"No." Lindsey glanced away, not meeting his gaze.

"Hey, don't pay any attention to my family. They get a kick out of teasing everyone. Sometimes their humor isn't all that funny, though. I swear they're harmless."

The elevator doors opened and they stepped off on the third floor. Lindsey nodded, but didn't say anything else as they entered the ICU.

Alice was there, sitting in a chair next to Abe's bed, but Austin's gaze zeroed in on his dad, who still looked pale against the sheets. The breathing tube was out and there seemed to be less equipment in the room, he noted with a sense of relief.

Maybe his dad was doing better after all.

"Hi, Mom. Dad, how are you feeling?" he asked, approaching the bed.

"Better, now that the breathing tube is out," Abe grumbled in a hoarse voice. "That tube was the worst part of the surgery."

His dad's chest had been cut open, his heart had been operated on, yet his biggest complaint was the breathing tube? Austin hid a grin. No doubt he hadn't liked the breathing tube because it had kept him from talking.

"As you can see, he's back to his cranky self," his mother added.

"Introduce me to your friend," Abe said, his gaze resting on Lindsey.

"Dad, I'd like you to meet Lindsey Winters." He took Lindsey's arm and drew her close to his father's bedside. "Lindsey, this is my father, Abe."

"It's nice to meet you," Lindsey said. "And I'm so glad you're feeling better."

"Me, too." Abe grimaced. "Although they're not letting me go to a regular floor until tomorrow."

"Tomorrow?" Austin frowned. "That seems way too soon."

"Not really," Lindsey pointed out. "They usually try to get open-heart patients out of the ICU within twenty-four to forty-eight hours.

Your dad will be a day and a half post-op once he leaves here."

"That's exactly what Cleo, his nurse, said, too," his mother confirmed with a serene nod.

"Hmm." Maybe so, but he still didn't like it. What if his dad took a turn for the worse out on the floor? What if he suffered some sort of complication?

"It'll be OK, Austin," Lindsey murmured, putting a reassuring hand on his arm as if she'd read his troubled thoughts. "He'll be on telemetry when they do send him out, so they'll be able to watch his heart closely."

"I hope so," he said on a sigh, grateful Lindsey was there to help keep him grounded. Her knowledge as a nurse far exceeded his paramedic training, so he felt better knowing she wasn't worried about his dad going to the general floor.

He chatted with his parents for a few more minutes, but then sensed his dad was getting tired. "Dad, we're going to go back downstairs so you can get some rest." He glanced at his mother. "Mom, you've been up here all morning. Don't you think you should take a break? It's almost time for lunch."

His mother nodded. "I'll be down in a little while," she said.

As they walked back to the elevators, Lindsey glanced at him. "I feel awkward, being here with you, Austin. Maybe now that your dad is doing better, Josh and I should go home."

His footsteps faltered. "Please, don't go yet. Is my family really that overwhelming?"

"A little." She smiled, but it seemed a bit forced. "But your family is fine, really. I'm not overwhelmed, I just don't want to intrude. I guess there's no rush to leave."

"Thanks," he murmured, giving her hand a quick squeeze. He didn't want Lindsey to leave. She belonged there, with him and with his family. "I really appreciate you staying here with me."

They hadn't had a chance to talk since the night

they made love, but he vowed to talk to her soon. Lindsey needed to know how much he cared.

Somehow he had to let her know he wanted her around, permanently.

Lindsey followed Austin back down to the family center, not sure if she was doing the right thing by staying with him in Milwaukee or not.

Still, she couldn't bring herself to leave, not when he'd asked her so nicely to stay. Even though she felt like a fraud, she really did love being treated as a part of the family.

Josh and Ben were still playing video games but her stomach growled, betraying her hunger. They hadn't had much for breakfast, just a quick bagel that seemed like hours ago.

Luckily, everyone else was hungry, too. She pried Josh away from the video games as they made plans for lunch.

The Monroe clan trooped down to the hospital cafeteria together, the guys arguing over who was going to pick up the tab. In the end, they all threw a bunch of twenties into Adam's hand and he paid the bill, no doubt making up the difference out of his own pocket.

Lindsey found herself seated between Jillian and Abby, with Alaina and Krista directly across from her. Austin was at the other end of the table, next to the kids. She thought it was very clever the way the women maneuvered the kids to be near the men, shifting the parental responsibility just a bit.

In her opinion, it was good for the guys to share in the task of child rearing. Sam had been a good father to Josh, but he'd pretty much left most of the discipline and involvement in school to her.

When Austin got up from his seat to help cut up Ben's food for him, she found herself wondering what sort of father he'd be. If he took after his father, he'd be a great one.

"Ben looks a lot like Austin," she mused, noting the stark family resemblance.

"In looks, yes, but hopefully not in temperament," Alaina said with a frown. "At least, I hope not. Austin got into a lot of trouble when he was young."

"He did?" For some reason that surprised her. She'd known about Austin's womanizing reputation, but she'd always thought him very responsible.

"Absolutely." Abby flashed a wicked grin as she joined the conversation. "I could tell you about the time he held a party at our neighbor's house when they weren't home because he had a key to go inside and water the woman's plants. Or maybe you'd rather hear about the time he hitchhiked down to Chicago because he wanted to see a rock concert but my parents had grounded him. Or maybe—"

"Stop!" Lindsey held up a hand, trying not to laugh. "Really? He did all that?" She shot Alice, the matriarch of the family who sat at the head of the table, an awed look. "Your mother must be a saint."

"She is," Abby agreed. "Although only the boys gave her grief. I'm the angel of the family."

"No you're not," Alaina interrupted. "I was."

"The only thing I remember about Austin was that he had a different girlfriend every week during high school," Krista, Adam's fiancée, interjected in a dry tone. "All the girls mooned over him."

"Yeah, well, that hasn't changed," Alaina pointed out.

Lindsey had to agree. Just walking through the cafeteria, several women's gazes had followed Austin. She frowned, glancing at Austin's sisters. "So Austin hasn't ever had a serious relationship?"

"Nope." Abby rolled her eyes. "At least, not for lack of trying. He'd always been a bit of a loner, going out with lots of women but not really getting close to any of them."

"I see," Lindsey said, her stomach clenching as she lost her appetite. So much for her theory that Austin had been seriously burnt by a woman in the past.

"Do you?" Alaina challenged with a raised brow. "Because, honestly, Lindsey, you're the first woman he's ever introduced to the family. Ever."

Shocked by the news, she could only gape. "The first?"

"Yes, the first," Abby agreed. "So even though you haven't been seeing him long, we were hoping you were the one that would bring him to his knees."

"Abby!" Jillian said in a shocked tone. "That's not very nice."

"Hey, he's the one known around town as the heartbreaker, not me." Abby raised her hand in defense. "I just think it would be nice to meet the woman who finally brings my brother down."

As Austin's family laughed and joked, Lindsay felt worse and worse. She knew that everything they said was true, and not meant in a vengeful way at all, but hearing about Austin's reputation in detail certainly wasn't making her feel any better.

Abby had called him a heartbreaker.

Why would a loner heartbreaker suddenly want to saddle himself with a wife and son?

Very simply, he wouldn't. Her heart ached and

she realized just how much she'd been hoping maybe he'd changed.

She'd be better off resigning herself to the fact that her one night with Austin had been just that, one night.

The next day was spent very much the same, visiting with his family. Now that his father was doing better, the constant family time was starting to wear on Austin. He wished he and Lindsey could have more time alone. They still hadn't had much time to talk.

They'd been forced to wait much longer than usual down in the family center, until his father had been settled in a private room on a regular telemetry floor. Even then, they couldn't go visit right away as he'd gone for some sort of test. It wasn't until much later in the evening that Austin and Lindsey were able to go up and see him.

At least Lindsey hadn't talked any more about leaving to return home without him.

He didn't quite understand why Lindsey had

been so anxious to leave, unless Abby had said something to her. From what he could tell, she was getting along great with his family. In fact, he would have liked nothing more than to have introduced Lindsey as his fiancée. He'd blown his last proposal to her, but that had been because he'd blurted it out without any warning.

Now that he knew she'd been planning to divorce Sam, he was confident he could win her over.

Adam continued to give him a hard time, payback for when he'd flirted with Krista right under his nose. Austin couldn't really blame him. Adam and Krista certainly looked happy together.

The way he felt around Lindsey.

He glanced at her as they rode the elevators up to the third floor, where his father's room was located. Her expression was serious and he wondered what was going through her mind.

When the elevator doors opened, Austin held his arm in front of the electronic eye so she could pass through first. She thanked him with a smile, then fell into step beside him as he headed to his dad's room.

"Hi, Dad," he said, as they walked in. Finding himself eye to eye with his father made him stop abruptly. "Hey, look at you—up and walking around."

Abe made a wry face. "The nurses forced me to."

"That's because it's good for your heart, Mr Monroe," Lindsey said with a smile. "You're doing a great job, though."

"Still have the strength of a mouse," he muttered, sitting down in a chair next to his bed with a small groan. "But I'll be glad to go home."

"By the way, Mom will be back in about an hour or so," Austin informed him. His mother had been at his father's bedside almost non-stop during his hospitalization. "She ran home to take care of Murphy. We offered to take care of the dog for her, but I think she needed a break."

Abe's grumpy expression softened. "She deserves a break after the way I scared her with this stupid heart thing."

Had scared all of them. "Yeah, you really did that on purpose, didn't you?" Austin said in a dry tone. "She's fine. You guys will be back home, spoiling your grandchildren, before you know it."

"Speaking of grandchildren, I hear Lindsey has a son named Josh." The older man's gaze zeroed in on her. "Why haven't I met this young man?"

"I…uh…" Helplessly she looked at Austin. "No reason. You can meet him. He's downstairs entertaining Ben."

"Next time bring him with you," Abe commanded. Then he winced and put a hand over his heart. "Damn, I feel like I've run a marathon rather than just walked up and down the hall a couple of times."

The way Abe's face had grown pale bothered Austin. Lindsey stepped forward and took his dad's wrist in her fingers. "Let me check your pulse."

He glanced up, but there was no cardiac monitor in the room. "Lindsey?" Austin said, trying to hide his worry.

"Your heart is a little irregular, Mr Monroe." Lindsey said in a calm tone. "I think we'd better get you back into bed."

"I'm fine," he protested, but he leaned forward and pushed up from the chair to do as she asked.

He swayed and nearly toppled over. Austin rushed forward to grab his dad's arm when it looked like he might not make it. Between them, he and Lindsey managed to get him back into bed.

"I'm going to call the nurse," Lindsey said, pushing the button on the call light beside him. Austin didn't argue. His dad's skin was cool and clammy. Without a stethoscope, he could only imagine what his heart rate was.

"What's wrong?" Austin asked, in a low tone. "PVCs? V-tach? What?"

"Nothing that dramatic," she assured him. "If I had to guess I'd say he went into atrial fib. Very common for patients after undergoing open-heart surgery."

The nurse came into the room, lugging a portable monitor with her. Austin suspected his dad's abnormal heart rhythm had been picked up on the remote telemetry monitoring.

Abe lay back on his pillow, his eyes closed, his usually ruddy skin pale.

"Mr Monroe?" The nurse, Irene, leaned close. "Are you all right?"

"I don't feel so good," he said, keeping his eyes closed. "Dizzy."

Austin was very thankful they'd gotten him back into bed when they had. At the moment Abe looked like he might need a trip back to the ICU. He watched as Irene connected Abe to the portable monitor and then proceeded to check his blood pressure. Within moments she was paging the doctor.

"Let's try some Metropolol," the doctor ordered when he came into the room a few minutes later. Austin caught a glimpse of the guy's name on his badge—Dr R. Gaines. He remembered him as his dad's cardiothoracic surgeon. "Did he get his scheduled beta-blocker dose this morning?"

"No, the nurse said his blood pressure was too low," Irene explained.

Dr Gaines's clenched jaw told Austin his opinion of that, but the doctor didn't say anything more. Austin understood the doctor's frustration, though. He'd read an article at the paramedic base describing the importance of beta-blockers post cardiac surgery and the problems some nurses caused by being too cautious in giving the medication.

Beta-blocker medication was supposed to be held back if the patient's blood pressure or pulse was too low but, normally, the article suggested the nurse should wait an hour and check the vital signs again after the patient had been up, moving around. Otherwise holding back the dose for a lengthy time could result in irregular heart rhythms. Like atrial fibrillation.

"Get the defibrillator ready in case this doesn't work," Dr Gaines said in an authoritative tone. "We may have to cardiovert."

Damn. "I'd better call my mother," Austin

muttered, knowing she'd never forgive him if something happened.

"Just wait a minute," Lindsey cautioned, placing her hand on his arm. He wanted to haul her close. "Let's see if the medication works, all right?"

Sweat beaded on Abe's brow. He looked awful, as if his body definitely didn't like the irregular heart rhythm. Irene left and returned moments later with the entire crash cart, the defibrillator sitting on top.

Austin tensed when he saw the crash cart. He clung to Lindsey's hand as he stared at the heart monitor, watching the irregular beats of Abe's heart and praying his rhythm would convert.

It didn't.

"Cardiovert with 50 joules," Dr Gaines said.

Lindsey pulled Austin out of the way.

"Charging." Irene slapped the patches on Abe's chest, before turning back to the defibrillator. "All clear?" She waited a moment for everyone to step back from the bed before hitting the button.

Abe's body gave a little jump when she delivered the shock.

For an agonizing moment his heart paused, then returned to its normal rhythm.

Austin breathed a prayer of thanks, but his hands were still shaking.

It had been a close call. Too close. Clearly, his dad wasn't out of the woods yet.

CHAPTER TWELVE

AUSTIN was exhausted by the time they left the hospital. He'd called his mom, who had hurried in to see what had happened. There had been a lot of discussion between the nurse and Dr. Gaines, but in the end they'd decided not to move his dad back to the ICU.

Austin wasn't sure if that was a good thing or not. At least in the ICU they'd be watching him more closely.

"Is your dad going to be OK?" Josh asked, when they finally climbed into the rental car.

"He's going to be fine," Austin assured the boy, although he wished he felt as confident. He caught Lindsey's gaze and his heart squeezed when she smiled at him.

He couldn't imagine going through all this without Lindsey. Even during the crisis at his dad's bedside, Lindsey had been there, supporting him.

Wishing they didn't have to stay in separate hotel rooms, Austin drove back down the street. Since they'd already grabbed a meal earlier in the cafeteria, there was no reason to delay going back.

Inside the hotel, Josh ran down the hall to his and Lindsey's room, the magnetic key in his hand. Austin and Lindsey followed more slowly.

"Are you sure you're going to be all right?" she asked in a low tone. "You've been through a lot."

He wanted to ask her to stay with him, but knew she couldn't, not with Josh sharing a room with her. He forced a smile. "Thanks. But I'm fine. Really. Do you have a quick minute to change my dressing?"

"Sure." Since the back-rub incident, Lindsey hadn't spent any more time than necessary in changing the dressing over his wound, her touch professional and impersonal, as if he were just another patient. This time was no different. Once she was finished, she stepped back. "You're all set. The area looks like it's healing well."

"Good." He put his shirt back on and turned toward the door.

She gave his arm a slight squeeze as he headed out to his own room. "Good night. See you in the morning."

"Good night, Lindsey." He fought the urge to crush her close, kissing her until they were both blind with desire, but he forced himself to leave, closing her hotel room door behind him.

For a moment he leaned his forehead on the doorframe, wishing things were different. Holding his desire in check with Josh around wasn't easy. They'd been in Milwaukee for two days, but still hadn't had their chance to talk. As much as he loved his family, there wasn't a moment of alone time, between his siblings, their spouses and children, not to mention Josh.

Maybe he could persuade Alec or Alaina to

watch Josh tomorrow night so he and Lindsey could go out for dinner. A nice romantic meal. He was chagrined to realize they'd never really had a date. Not the two of them alone. Without Josh.

Shaking his head at his idiocy, he used his key card to get into his own room. Inside, he glanced at the adjoining door separating their rooms, which was shut.

He didn't test it but he was pretty sure it was locked, too.

Tossing his shirt on the chair, he stretched out on the bed, being careful of his back dressing, and stared at the blank television screen.

He should probably try to watch something to take his mind off his troubles, because there was no way he was going to fall asleep anytime soon.

Lindsey had trouble falling asleep, but must have dozed a little because a noise woke her up and the small alarm clock on the bedside stand read a quarter after twelve.

She could hear Josh's even breathing from the bed next to hers. She stared into the darkness wondering what had woken her up.

Then she heard it again, a thump and a muttered curse. Austin? A few more thumps from the room next door had her getting up out of bed, shivering in her thin pajamas and making her way to the door separating their rooms.

Feeling foolish, she pressed her ear to the door, straining to listen. She heard a voice, but the voice sounded deep, like Austin's, not the muted sounds of the television.

Was he talking to someone in his family? Had his father's condition changed? She wouldn't be at all surprised to discover the staff at Trinity had ended up moving him to the ICU.

Biting her lip, she reached up and flipped the lock of the connecting door to unlatch it and then twisted the door handle, half expecting the door to be locked.

It wasn't. Grateful she didn't have to take a chance on waking Josh by knocking, she slipped through the opening and peered into Austin's room.

He stood next to his bed, wearing only a pair of flannel pants and no shirt as he spoke on the phone with the hospital. She must have made a noise because he swiveled around and looked at her.

"OK, let me know if anything changes. Thanks, Abby." He snapped his phone shut and came toward her. "Lindsey? What's wrong? Trouble sleeping?"

"You're the one who's not sleeping." She kept her voice low and carefully shut the connecting door between the rooms so Josh wouldn't hear them. "I heard you bumping into things. What happened? Your dad?"

"He's fine." Austin's gaze trailed over her and she crossed her arms over her chest, knowing her baggy pajamas were hardly sexy. Heck, she was sharing a room with her son. Sexy wasn't an option. "I'm sorry I woke you. I just wanted to check on him."

"I understand." She wished there was something she could do; he wore his worry like a heavy winter coak. But despite Abe's health, there were always potential complications after surgery, especially major open-heart surgery. "Maybe you should take something to help you sleep."

Austin shook his head. "No, thanks. But I could use a hug."

The flash of vulnerability in his gaze caught her off guard. A hug was a simple request. How could she refuse? He obviously hadn't been getting much rest. Two steps found her in his arms, her face buried in the crick of his neck, his face nuzzling her hair.

"I was so worried about him, but you were so calm when you checked his pulse," Austin murmured in her ear. "I'm glad you called the nurse when you did. Have I thanked you for coming?"

Her heart swelled as she smiled against him. "Yes." She held him close and then loosened her grip, intending to step back.

He didn't let her go. Caught within the circle

of his arms, she glanced up to find him staring down at her intently. Before she could ask him what was wrong, he bent his head and kissed her.

As before, his kiss instantly melted her resistance. He kissed her with a hunger mixed with desperation, as if he was afraid she'd run if he let her go.

The problem was that she didn't feel at all like running.

His mouth was sweet, gentle but probing as he took his time tasting her. Even though it had only been a few days since they'd made love, it seemed like forever since they'd been together.

"Lindsey, I need you so much," he whispered between kisses. His hands moved restlessly over her thin yet baggy pajamas. "Please, stay, just for a while."

She caught her breath, wanting nothing more. His sisters had claimed he hadn't ever brought a woman home to meet them. Maybe he did see her differently. Her heart thrilled at the possibility. Yet she hesitated, thinking about Josh.

Her son had seemed fine, but what if he woke up from a nightmare? Or was sick again?

"Do you want to check on Josh first?" he asked, guessing the source of her inner debate.

"Yes, just for a moment."

He loosened his arms and she stepped away on shaky legs. Steeling her resolve, she eased open the connecting door and peered in on her son. He was sprawled on the bed, dead to the world.

Closing the door with a soft click, she turned back to Austin. He stood right where she'd left him, not taking anything for granted. He was so gorgeous, so all-encompassing male, he literally stole her breath.

She didn't want to think about what the potential consequences might be of a second night of lovemaking with the infamous heartbreaker Monroe. Right now there was nothing that could make her walk away from him.

"Lindsey, I love you." Her heart quickened when he carefully cupped her face in his hands and pressed his mouth against hers in a soft kiss.

"You do?" she gasped, hardly able to believe him. Did he really mean it? She was afraid to hope. She wanted to tell him how much she loved him, too, but couldn't say the words even though she felt them in her heart.

"Yes. Let me show you how much." When he kissed her again, she wanted to believe this was the start of a real relationship. Not a rebound romance, like the kind her mother excelled at, but a very real, based-on-love relationship.

When he gently unbuttoned the ugly, shapeless pajama jacket, she didn't stop him. Not even when he raked a hungry gaze over her, her breasts bared in the dim light he'd left burning next to the bed.

When he'd tugged off her pants, he gently lifted her up and set her on the bed.

"The light," she whispered, when he'd discarded his flannel pants and gathered her close, pressing her against him.

"I want to see you," he said in a low voice. "You're so beautiful, Lindsey."

She wasn't, there were faint stretch marks on

her lower abdomen, thanks to Josh, but she suddenly felt beautiful when he trailed kisses down her throat to the valley between her breasts.

And then lower still.

Drowning in pleasure, she hung on to his shoulders, enjoying every stroke of his tongue, ever murmured compliment. When the pleasure built to a level she could barely stand, he sheathed himself with a condom and slid deep, taking her even higher.

He moved, slowly at first then faster, bringing wave after wave of desire shuddering through her, until she thought her body would shatter beneath the pressure.

"Austin!" she cried, muffling the sound against his shoulder the best she could.

"I love you," he said on a gasp, when he followed her over the edge.

Breathless and satiated, the haze slowly cleared from her mind as he cuddled her close.

She loved him, too. This time she was convinced she hadn't confused lust and love. Not when her whole body tingled from Austin's touch. She hated to admit she loved him more than she'd ever loved Sam. She'd been so young when she'd met Sam. Having become pregnant with Josh had forced them into an earlier marriage than they'd planned.

Austin was different than Sam. In so many ways.

Yet a smidgen of doubt remained. Austin had been playing the field for so long, she found it hard to believe he'd really meant what he'd said.

How was it possible that he'd suddenly fallen in love with her? If so, why? How in the world was she any different from all the other women he'd ever loved and left?

She drifted off in a semisleep state for a while, but when Austin's breathing slowed and deepened, she knew it was time to return to her own room.

Regretfully, she slid out from under his arm, inching toward the edge of the bed. It wasn't far because Austin took up more than his share of space.

Lightning fast, he grabbed her wrist, suddenly wide-awake. "Don't go."

His quickness startled her. "I have to," she said, pulling the sheet up over her bare breasts. Where in the heck had she left her pajamas? "Josh will wonder where I am. I have to be there when he wakes up in the morning."

Austin let out a heavy sigh, let her go and tunneled his fingers through his hair and nodded. "I know."

She saw her pajama pants and tried to grab them with her toes.

"Lindsey, I asked you before and I haven't changed my mind, so I'm asking you again. Will you marry me?"

She sucked in a harsh breath, her heart pounding in her chest. He might have asked her once out of a misguided sense of wanting to help her, but twice? She didn't know what to think. "Why? Out of all the women you've dated in the past, why do you want to marry me?"

His expression turned uncertain. "So my sisters

did say something to upset you. I'm sorry, Lindsey. I can't lie to you. I haven't lived the life of a monk. There have been women, but none of them meant anything to me."

No kidding. That much she'd figured out by his reputation alone. She just couldn't believe he suddenly felt differently now. "Sam always claimed you never dated the same woman more than once. I think in some ways he was jealous, because he was stuck with me."

Austin's gaze darkened. "Is that why you won't marry me? Because of Sam?"

"Not exactly." She tugged the sheet higher, overly conscious of her nakedness. If she was honest, she'd admit that her marriage breakdown was a big part of her concern. She couldn't bear the thought of going from one bad relationship to another. "My marriage with Sam was about to end. I told you, I filed for divorce the day before he left to go on that last smoke jumping mission." No matter what Austin said, she still felt Sam's death was partially her fault.

"Lindsey, there's something you need to know. I should have told you before." He paused, seeming to search for the right words. "Sam's death wasn't your fault. It was mine."

"Yours?" She didn't believe him.

"Yeah." He dragged his gaze to hers, his expression grim. "I'm sorry. I should have told you the truth a long time ago."

"What?" She didn't understand what he was talking about. Smoke jumping was dangerous, that much she knew, but Austin wasn't the reckless sort, not in the way Sam sometimes was.

Truthfully, she would have trusted Austin with her life.

"That day, we were fighting the wildfire under dicey conditions. We were warned going in that the wind might shift, but they were predicting we had a good twelve hours before that happened."

She made a small sound, urging him to continue.

"We were making headway against the fire. Sam was working north of me when suddenly the wind shifted, coming up from the south. He was farther away in the clear, but I wasn't. The fire was heading straight toward me. I figured my time was up, but Sam appeared out of nowhere, telling me to run for the river. Even after we got to the river, Sam didn't quit. He kept on working, lighting a backfire to divert the path of the wildfire. When he finally finished, we both jumped into the water. The fire didn't get us, but he must have taken in more smoke than I did because suddenly his breathing wasn't so good."

She couldn't speak, the picture he painted was far too real. Good heavens, she'd never realized how close Austin had come to dying, too.

"He'd inhaled too much smoke, but there was nowhere for us to go. I called for the medevac chopper to come and get us, but it was too late." Austin's gaze was tortured. "He could have saved himself, Lindsey, but he didn't. Because he came back for me. And he died for his efforts."

She didn't know what to say. After all these months, she had honestly believed Sam had been careless. Had purposefully put his life on the line because she'd filed for divorce and had asked him to leave.

For months she'd built him up in her mind as being the bad guy. Especially after she'd discovered the mountain of debt he'd left. And she'd been angry at the way he'd tossed away his life, as if she and Josh hadn't been worth the effort.

Now Austin had just told her that in the final moments of his life Sam hadn't been careless after all.

He'd been a hero.

CHAPTER THIRTEEN

LINDSEY stared at him for a long moment, not sure what to say. Truthfully, she was a little glad to hear that in the end Sam had come through when it had counted.

"Can you forgive me, Lindsey?" Austin's tone held a note of anxiety. "I know I should have told you sooner, but I didn't want you to hate me."

"Of course I don't hate you, Austin." She pressed her lips together in a self-deprecating frown. "How odd we've both been feeling guilty over the same thing."

"His last thoughts were of you," Austin said slowly. "He was worried about both you and Josh."

What was left of her anger evaporated. Sam

may not have been the best husband, but he had cared. "Thanks for telling me."

The expectant look he gave her made her realize she'd never answered his question about marriage. As much as she wanted to, she just couldn't. Not yet. Everything was just too confusing.

"I don't know if I can marry you, Austin," she finally admitted. "My heart wants to say yes, but my head is telling me I need time."

His smile was crooked. "So listen to your heart."

She let out a half-hearted chuckle. "I'll think about it, OK? I promise I'll consider your proposal."

Expecting an argument, she was somewhat surprised when he nodded. "That's all I'm asking, Lindsey."

She glanced around, relieved that he wasn't pushing the issue. "I, um, need my pajamas."

His sexy, knowing grin was almost enough to entice her to stay. "I'll get them."

Ignoring his nakedness, he climbed from the bed and fetched her pajamas. He was beautiful, his hard muscular body very impressive. She was embarrassed to discover her pajama top was on one side of the room, but her bottoms had been flung onto a chair on the opposite side of the room.

Good grief, how had they gotten way over there?

"Thanks," she murmured, when he handed her the clothing. Trying to preserve her modesty wasn't easy, but she managed to slip the pajamas back on. At the same time Austin had retrieved his drawstring flannel pants.

He stopped her before she made her way back through the connecting door. "Lindsey?"

"Yes?"

He didn't answer but pulled her back into his arms for a thorough kiss.

Her head was spinning by the time he let her go. "I'll see you tomorrow," he murmured.

"Uh-huh." After reminding herself she couldn't stay, no matter how tempted she was, she took a deep breath and sneaked back into the room she was sharing with Josh.

He was still sleeping, thank heavens.

She slipped into her own bed and stared at the ceiling, mulling over Austin's proposal.

Somehow it was difficult to remember the reasons she'd resisted saying yes.

The next day, Josh was up early. Of course, he'd gotten a full night of sleep, unlike some people in the room.

Stifling a wide yawn, Lindsay padded to the tiny coffeemaker, filled it with water and stared as the carafe slowly filled with freshly brewed coffee.

The stupid machine dripped slower than molasses.

She'd finished two cups before she felt ready to face the day, hence they were later than usual for their normal breakfast routine.

Josh had found Austin's room and with a guilty start she remembered she hadn't completely closed the connecting door between their rooms, and she pasted a smile on her face as she walked in. "Good morning. Are we ready for breakfast?"

"Yeah!" Josh was practically bouncing on the

bed he had so much energy. "Guess what, Mom? Austin says I'm going to go over to Mrs Moore's house tonight for dinner."

"Mrs Moore?" she echoed with a frown, sliding a questioning glance at Austin.

"My sister Alaina is having all the kids over for a pizza dinner," Austin explained. "I figured you wouldn't mind."

She didn't actually mind, but he could have asked her first.

"This way, you and Austin can go out for a fancy-smantzy dinner." Josh comically rolled his eyes, making a goofy face, and flopped back on the bed. "No kids allowed."

"Thanks for letting the cat out of the bag," Austin muttered.

"Cat?" Josh sat up and frowned. "What cat?"

"Never mind." So Austin had created this kid dinner just so they could go out? She couldn't help being impressed at his ingenuity. "Let's eat, shall we?"

Josh chatted through breakfast, which was a

good thing because after spending the night with Austin she was finding it difficult to get back on normal terms. Maybe it was just her imagination, but she was sure he kept sending her smoldering glances that promised more passion.

She swallowed hard and concentrated on her food.

When they'd finished eating, Austin drove them over to the hospital. The plan was to visit for a while, then go back to his parents' house to help get things ready for Abe to return home.

They chatted in the waiting room with the other family members as there were too many of them to descend on Abe at one time. Lindsey leaned over to Austin.

"You might want to arrange for subs or something for lunch," she warned, "because otherwise your mother is going to feel as if she needs to feed us all."

"Good point." Austin turned to Abby and arranged for a party sub to be ordered and delivered around noon.

Despite his arrhythmia episode the previous evening, Abe looked fine when they made their way up to visit. This time she took Josh with her so he could meet Austin's father.

"Mr Monroe, this is my son, Josh. Josh, this is Mr Monroe, Austin's father."

"You can call me Grandpa Monroe if you like," Abe confided. He was sitting up in a chair, dressed in a striped hospital gown and robe. "That's what the other grandkids call me."

Josh glanced at her and she gave a subtle nod, granting her permission. Easier than using "Mr Monroe" with so many other Mr Monroes around.

"So what grade are you in at school?" Abe asked.

Josh went into a discussion of what was currently happening in the fourth grade, and of course mentioned the Tai Kwon Do classes he and his friend Tony were taking. Which led to a demonstration of his yellow belt "form."

As Josh moved through his choreographed moves, Lindsey had to admit she was impressed.

Maybe Austin was right about the martial arts being all about self-control.

Heck, maybe she should learn some self-control herself.

"You're not upset about dinner tonight, are you?" Austin asked, after they'd returned to the waiting room.

"No, although I was taken aback at first," she answered honestly. "But it was sweet of you to make the arrangements."

Austin's grin faded a bit. "I'm sorry it took me so long to realize we'd never really been out on a date by ourselves."

She shrugged. "Dating isn't easy as a single mom."

He nodded, but she could tell he was still troubled by the lapse. They made their way over to his parents' house, where much of the family had already congregated.

Lindsey ended up helping to throw together some ready-made casseroles to make things easier for Austin's mother, while the guys worked on setting up a room for Abe on the first floor so he wouldn't have to negotiate the steep staircase leading to the master bedroom on the second floor. The kids were relegated to play in the family room, basically to stay out of everyone's way.

"Darn it, the kitchen sink is blocked again," Abby said in exasperation. "Lindsey, will you go and ask Austin to come and look at it?"

"Sure." Feeling as if there were too many cooks in the kitchen anyway, she was glad to escape. Austin's family was nice, but they made a simple project into a major production.

She found Abby's husband, Nick, and Alec in the downstairs bedroom, putting the bed frame together. "Where's Austin?" she asked.

"Upstairs with Adam." Alec flashed a grin. "Take a right at the top of the stairs."

"Thanks." She followed his simple directions but her steps slowed as she neared the top of the stairs.

Austin's voice came through the doorway loud and clear.

"Knock it off, Adam. I know what I'm doing. I promised Sam I'd take care of Lindsey and Josh. I can handle a little responsibility."

She sucked in a harsh breath. Responsibility? Was that really how he viewed her and Josh—as a responsibility?

Because he'd promised Sam he'd take care of them?

Dazed and nauseous, she turned away and stumbled into the nearest room, which just happened to be the bathroom. She sank onto the commode before her knees gave out.

Why hadn't she put the pieces together before?

Austin had never been in a serious relationship. For years he'd hopped from one woman to the next, leaving a string of broken hearts in his wake.

He could have any woman he wanted.

Why would a serious heartbreaker suddenly decide to settle down with a wife and son?

Because he'd made a promise to his best friend.

Austin was so intent on marrying her because

he felt he needed to keep his promise to take care of her and Josh.

It made so much sense now that she put it all together.

And the stark truth made her want to cry.

Lindsey could barely paste a smile on her face for Austin's family, but the chaos over lunch helped her to hide her feelings.

But she couldn't stay. Especially not when Austin had planned a special dinner for them. And when he drove off to buy a new elbow pipe for the kitchen sink, she took her chance and ran.

Not literally, but she did manage to call a cab.

"Tell Austin I had to go back to the hotel for a while," she said to Abby when she wanted to know where they were going. "I'm not feeling well."

"Is there anything I can do to help?" Abby asked with a worried frown. "I'm sure Alaina wouldn't mind keeping an eye on Josh if you want to catch a nap."

"No, we'll be fine." The last thing she wanted

to do was to leave Josh with Alaina. Not when she had every intention of packing up their belongings and heading out to the airport to catch the first plane to LA. Luckily, Austin had purchased electronic tickets for them to fly standby, so she didn't need anything from him.

Least of all a marriage proposal because he felt responsible for her.

"Why are we leaving without Austin?" Josh asked, becoming stubborn when she told him to pack his things.

"Because I need to get back home for work." It was easier to stretch the truth than to explain the personal issues between them.

"You had a fight, didn't you?" Josh demanded in a petulant tone. "I'm not going. You can't make me."

Her temper snapped. "Yes, you are! You're my son and I'm telling you we're leaving. *Now.*"

The shocked expression on his face when she yelled at him haunted her on the sullen ride to the airport.

Her mother had always taken her frustrations about her failed relationships out on her.

She felt sick, knowing she was following in her mother's footsteps in more ways than one.

Austin swore under his breath as he managed to get the cracked pipe replaced under his mother's sink. At first it had simply been clogged, but in trying to get the pipe apart to clean it out, he'd cracked the darned thing, requiring a trip to the closest hardware store.

He crawled out from under the sink with a sigh of relief. One project finished. Maybe his brothers had moved all the furniture down from his dad's room in the hours he'd played plumber.

He cleaned up the mess and looked around for Lindsey. It was later than he'd thought, almost four in the afternoon. She wasn't in the family room with the kids. And neither was Josh.

After wandering through the various rooms in his parents' house, he discovered she seemed to have disappeared.

"Abby?" He cornered the sister Lindsey seemed to talk to the most. "Have you seen Lindsey and Josh?"

"Oh, yeah, I was supposed to tell you she went back to the hotel right after lunch. I guess she wasn't feeling well."

What? Since when? "How did she get there?" He'd had the rental car to run to the hardware store.

"I think she called a cab." Abby frowned. "Although now that you mention it, I don't know why she didn't just ask for a ride. Any one of us could have taken her back. Is everything all right?"

He had a bad feeling things weren't all right. "I don't know. I'm going to go back to the hotel to check on her."

Abby's worried expression cleared. "Good idea. Maybe the full extent of the Monroe family got too much for her. You said she doesn't have any family of her own. We are a bit much to digest all at one time."

"Yeah. Maybe." Funny, Lindsey hadn't mentioned feeling overwhelmed by his family. Instead, he would have thought just the opposite. She seemed to enjoy having his sisters to talk to.

He made it back to the hotel in record time, a mere fifteen minutes later. He went to Lindsey's room and rapped on the door.

A man opened the door. "Yeah?"

Embarrassed, he stepped back. "Sorry, wrong room."

He spun around and marched back to the front desk. No, Lindsey Winters hadn't requested to be moved to a different room. She'd checked out a couple of hours ago.

He couldn't believe it. She'd left. She'd left! Without him. Without saying a word. Had he pushed too hard? She'd said she'd consider his proposal. What had gone wrong?

In a daze he returned to his room. There was a hotel envelope with his name on it propped against the TV.

He quickly read her note. "Josh and I are not your responsibility, Austin. I know you promised Sam you'd take care of us but, believe me, Josh and I will be fine on our own. Please, thank your family for me. Take care of yourself, Lindsey."

Responsibility? Promise to Sam? How in the heck had she learned about his deathbed promise to Sam?

Then he knew. He'd mentioned it to Adam. She must have overheard him. His older brother had been giving him a hard time as usual. Adam had said something about how he'd better not love and leave Lindsey because she deserved better. Annoyed at his brother's assumption, he'd told Adam he'd loved Lindsey for months and knew damn well what marriage was all about. He'd only told him about the promise he'd made because Adam hadn't taken him seriously.

Damn, he hadn't meant her to find out the way she had. He had promised Sam he'd take care of her and Josh, but that wasn't why he wanted to marry her. He wanted to marry her because he loved her.

He stared at the note. She didn't believe in his love, that much was clear. But what he didn't understand was why. He'd told her he loved her and wanted to marry her. Even if she had overheard his comments about his promise and responsibility, why had a snippet of conversation overridden what he'd told her?

What else could he say to convince her?

Or was the real problem that she didn't love him back?

Austin tossed his clothes into his suitcase. He wanted to go straight back to Sun Valley, but first he needed to explain to Alaina that Josh wouldn't be coming back and then he needed to see his dad one last time, just to make sure he was OK.

But, dammit, once he did get back home, he and Lindsey were going to have a long talk. Somehow she had to make her believe he loved her. She had to give them a chance.

Because he couldn't imagine spending the rest of his life without her.

Austin was exhausted when he finally trudged out to his car, which he'd left at the airport. Flying standby was a pain in the butt. He'd had to wait hours before he'd been able to find an available seat on a flight home. He hadn't seen Lindsey or Josh at the Milwaukee airport, so he could only assume they'd had better luck in finding a flight than he had.

As he drove home, he thought about what to say to Lindsey. How on earth could he get her to believe him? Not only had he told her he loved her but he'd done his best to show his love with action.

Making love with her had been amazing. Better than amazing. No woman had ever touched his heart the way she did. He couldn't believe she didn't feel anything for him in return.

His cell phone rang and he quickly glanced at it, hoping the caller was Lindsey. But, no, it was just his family. They'd figured out something was going on when he'd told them Lindsey and Josh had left to fly home.

He let the call go to voice mail. As much as he loved his family, he couldn't talk to them yet.

How could he, when he hadn't even spoken to Lindsey?

When he pulled up his driveway, the house was completely dark. For the second time that day his stomach clenched. It was only eight o'clock at night. Were they already in bed, sleeping?

He didn't bother with his luggage but threw the car into Park and jumped out. Opening the front door with his key, he flipped on the light and looked around.

No note. Was that good or bad? He didn't know.

There was no sign of Lindsey or Josh having been there, as he walked through the kitchen, into the living room and then down the hall toward the bedrooms.

When he opened the door to Lindsey's room, the bed was neatly made. When he walked over to the dresser and opened the drawers, they were completely empty.

The same went for Josh's room. Lindsey and Josh had packed up their things and moved out.

The message couldn't have been more clear.

Lindsey obviously believed their relationship was over.

CHAPTER FOURTEEN

LINDSEY drove a sulky Josh over to Tony's house as they were off school for the day, glad to have a little bit of breathing room from him. He'd been so upset with her, first because they'd left Milwaukee without Austin and then when she'd decided they were moving back home, despite the construction in progress.

"I'll pick you up at four," she told him when he jumped out of the car.

"Whatever." He didn't slam the door, but then again he wasn't his usual happy self either.

Back home, she glanced around her cottage with a feeling of satisfaction. When she'd woken up that morning she'd suffered a momentary pang at how she'd moved out of Austin's house last night, but now she was convinced it was for the best. When she'd gone through the mail from while she'd been gone, she'd discovered all the nurses at Sun Valley Hospital were getting a modest raise. Encouraged by the news, she did some household budget calculations based on her new salary.

If she was careful, she could pay the high-interest loan payment by working just one extra shift a pay period instead of two. Things weren't as bleak as she'd thought. In fact, it felt good to have a home of her own, one she could afford and be responsible for.

Crossing to the kitchen counter, she threw together a quick sandwich for lunch, trying to ignore the fine layer of drywall dust covering every surface. On the positive side, she'd discovered the electrical work to bring the wiring up to code was complete, so the house was safe to live in from that standpoint. There were still quite a few drywall repairs to be made, but there was no reason she and Josh couldn't stay there while the work was being done.

No one had ever died from eating drywall dust, had they? She gave her sandwich a dubious glance but then took a big bite.

Maybe living in a construction zone would be uncomfortable, but it certainly wasn't impossible.

And if it was lonely without Austin around, she'd get over it. So would Josh.

She sighed and put down her half-eaten sandwich. The impact on Josh of her rift with Austin was the toughest to take. No matter how hard she tried to tell herself they would have had to move home sooner or later, it wasn't easy. Josh was too important. He'd come so far, she didn't want to see him regress. Regardless of what had transpired between her and Austin, she needed to ask him if he'd keep in touch with Josh so her son didn't lose the connection to a positive male role model.

Josh deserved at least that much stability. And Austin wouldn't refuse, not when staying in touch with Josh would fulfill his promise to Sam. She swallowed hard. Surely making love to her had gone above and beyond the call of duty.

The front door to her house abruptly swung open with a bang. When Austin strode in, she jumped, knocking her glass of milk and spilling the contents onto her half-eaten dusty sandwich.

Steeling herself for an argument, she opened her mouth to try and explain, but he swept her into his arms and kissed her senseless.

His mouth wasn't rough or angry but deeply sensual. So much so it didn't take long for her to melt against him. Her head was spinning when he finally broke free.

"Are you really willing to throw this away?" he demanded.

She took a few steps away, grabbing onto the counter for support while trying to marshal her thoughts. Somehow she had to make him understand.

"Austin, the first man I married was out of obligation—because I was pregnant. It seemed the right thing at the time, especially because I thought I loved him." She sighed. "But things changed, and I figured out obligation isn't exactly a good foundation for marriage. I'm not going to make the same mistake again."

"Wait a minute. You're pregnant?" His eyes sparkled with blatant hope.

"No!" Good thing he wasn't within reach or she might have smacked him. "Of course not. Why would you think that?"

When he simply shrugged, she continued, "Listen to me. When my marriage to Sam fell apart, I knew it was because we didn't love each other enough." She thought about how Austin's parents had interacted during the time of crisis, the way his whole family pulled together. She wished she'd had that with Sam, or even with her own family. But she didn't. She hadn't even seen her mother since she'd left home and enrolled at nursing school. To say they weren't close was a gross understatement. "Sam and I didn't have what your parents have."

Austin was silent for a moment. "Maybe you did marry Sam because you were pregnant, but if it makes a difference, he never once said anything about it."

She had to admit she was surprised. The way Sam had chafed against the responsibilities of marriage toward the end, she would have thought he would have confided in his best friend. "I guess I'm glad he didn't say anything, but the result was the same."

"What result? What happened, Lindsey? Why did your marriage fall apart?" His earnest expression convinced her he really wanted to know.

She stared at Austin, wondering how to answer him. "There wasn't any specific incident, we just stopped loving each other." How could she make him understand something she didn't quite understand herself? "Don't you see? That's exactly the problem. There wasn't any one major thing. Heck, I didn't even know about his gambling problem until after he died." She drew a shaky hand through her hair. "He wasn't a horrible person, he didn't hit me or hurt me. But I didn't love him enough. And I wanted something more out of my life than an empty marriage."

"You deserve more out of life than an empty marriage," Austin agreed, a puzzled frown in his brow. "I wish I'd known about his debts, though."

"Me, too." Lindsey sighed. "It's embarrassing to admit, but I always let Sam take care of the bills. I guess it's one of the reasons I'm so determined to remain independent."

Austin looked surprised. "But I don't understand. How did he get so far into debt?"

"I don't know." She raised her gaze to his. "I think Sam was looking for something different, something to make up for what we didn't have in our marriage. I don't think he was happy—at least, not being married to me."

"I don't believe it," Austin said, shaking his head. "He never once said anything to me about not wanting to be married to you."

"Yet he envied your bachelor lifestyle," she felt compelled to point out.

Austin hesitated. "Maybe. But I know he cared for you, Lindsey. It could have been as simple as the two of you getting married too young."

"Maybe." She tried to smile. "But caring isn't enough. Marriage is hard enough without lack of love stacked against you."

Austin was silent for a moment. "You're right. Caring alone isn't enough."

She breathed a sigh of relief. He did understand after all. "I am right." She strove for a casual tone. "So now that you understand where I'm coming from, there's no reason we can't be friends. Right?"

Friends? Austin stared at her. He'd admired her from afar for years, had actually been jealous of Sam for having Lindsey as a wife, and she wanted to be friends?

Sam, the jerk, had put her deeply in debt.

And then that same jerk had turned around and saved *his* life.

Dammit. Lindsey was right. Maybe Sam's

heroic moment made up for the gambling. Either way, he couldn't feel guilty over the way Sam had saved his life.

But he hadn't asked Lindsey to marry him out of guilt. Or out of a sense of responsibility. He sure as heck hadn't asked her to marry him because of a deathbed promise.

"Lindsey, do you know why I've never been in a serious relationship?"

She gave a careless shrug. "So many women, so little time?"

Not funny. He narrowed his gaze. "No. Because of you. Do you remember when you and I first met?"

She quirked a brow. "Ah, you mean when you brought that overdose patient in who threw up charcoal all over me?"

"Yes." Maybe it wasn't glamorous but he remembered that day as if it were yesterday. Especially the keen disappointment when he'd caught sight of her wedding ring. He'd discovered later she'd only been married for just over a year then. If he'd met her first, before Sam, maybe things would have been different. For both of them. "You were so wonderful to work with, not arrogant or snooty, like some of the other nurses. Yes, that patient threw up all over you, but you weren't annoyed or disgusted. Instead, you were nothing but nice to me and to the rest of the paramedic crew."

"It wasn't your fault or the patient's fault he threw up on me," she protested. "Charcoal is supposed to make you throw up."

"True, but I was so impressed with your kindness and caring. The fact you were totally hot was a plus." He wasn't explaining himself well. "There was just something about you that called to me in a way no woman ever had done before. You have no idea how disappointed I was to discover you were married. I worked with Sam for months before I met you, but I didn't realize you belonged to him until the day Sam invited me over for dinner."

Lindsey looked so surprised by his revelation he

had to smile. That night, when he'd come over for dinner, he'd been poleaxed to realize his secret fantasy woman was actually married to his partner. Holding a coherent conversation with her had been a challenge. It had been the first time in his life he'd been envious of any of his friends.

"From that day on," he added, "I remember thinking Sam was the luckiest guy in the world."

"I never knew," she said in a low voice.

He snorted. "Of course you never knew. I wouldn't make a move on my friend's wife. I tried to get over my infatuation with you by dating other women." He grimaced, remembering those first few dates had ended badly. "It didn't work. Every time I got to know one of them, she couldn't compare to you. And when I went out on a paramedic call that needed a patient to be brought in to the Sun Valley ED, I always looked for you. Just seeing you, even from afar, was enough to make me smile."

"I don't believe it," she whispered.

"Lindsey, I never allowed myself to fall in love

with you, to even dream of having a chance with you, until Sam died. Yes, I promised him I'd take care of you and Josh. Why wouldn't I? There was nothing I wanted more than for the two of you to be safe and secure. It wasn't until I spent more time with you during those weeks after his death that I realized how much I loved you."

Then they'd had their fight, when he'd tried to tell her how to raise her son. She'd accused him of trying to run her life, and she'd been right. Staying away from her had been the hardest thing he'd ever done.

"Austin, I don't know what to say." Lindsey's gaze pleaded with him. "I'm shocked. All this time you never once hinted at any of this."

"If you don't feel the same way, that's fine." He forced himself to be diplomatic, not wanting to pressure her. "But, Lindsey, those nights we spent together, I could have sworn you felt something for me, too."

"I did. I do." She covered her face with her hands. "I don't know."

He took a deep breath. OK, he could somewhat understand her confusion. After all, this was a lot to comprehend at once. "Don't throw away what we have—please? Give us a chance."

Lindsey didn't know what to say. Or what to believe.

Austin claimed he loved her. Had always admired her. Had actually been jealous of Sam.

How odd that Sam had wanted Austin's bachelor lifestyle while Austin had wanted Sam's commitment.

She had to believe he was telling her the truth. His earnestness would have been impossible to fake. But what about her own feelings?

She'd thought she'd been in love with Sam, but those feelings changed. To be honest, she wasn't certain she'd ever really loved him at all.

What if her feelings for Austin weren't what she thought? Or worse, his feelings for her?

"Lindsey?" Austin was still waiting for an answer.

"I want to try again, Austin," she said slowly, "but you need to know, I'm scared."

"Scared?" He looked appalled. "Of me? I swear to you, Lindsey, I'd never do anything to hurt you or Josh. Never!"

She smiled. "Not of you, Austin. I'm afraid of ending up like my mother."

"Your mother?" he frowned. "I don't understand. I thought Sam told me your mother was dead."

"No, she just lives a lifestyle very different from mine. See, my dad walked out when I was five. Honestly, I hardly remember him. Apparently he wasn't around much. Anyway, after that my mother flew feetfirst into one bad relationship after another. Always for my benefit, of course, so we could eat and have nice clothes to wear. And I'd just get settled into one place when that relationship would end and we'd move into another."

"That must have been rough." He frowned. "Did any of these guys mistreat you?"

"No, nothing like that. It's just that I could tell

these guys were losers, even at a young age. I'd sworn to myself I'd never end up with a guy like that. Sam was a decent guy, seemed to really have his life together. I was impressed he was already a firefighter and paramedic. Heck, he was a hero in my eyes. But in the end, when I discovered the extent of our financial debt, I realized he had been more like the guys my mother hooked up with than I'd ever imagined."

"Lindsey." He stood, came around the table and drew her to her feet. "You're a nurse. You're wonderful with Josh. You're not your mother."

Hope flared. He was right, her mother's lack of steady work hadn't helped matters.

"I wish you could believe in me. In us. I know it's scary. Do you think I'm not scared? I don't want to mess things up either. Marriage is a lifelong commitment. All I can do is swear to you that I'll do whatever it takes to make you happy. I promise."

She wanted to believe him. Things were on track for her financially, so she didn't need

Austin's help there. Besides, her feelings for him were much deeper than that. Could she do this? Could she trust her feelings and take the leap? Looking into Austin's deep green eyes, she began to believe she could. Her smile was tremulous. "I want what your parents have. A marriage that is strong enough to last a lifetime."

He grinned, hope brightening his eyes. "Me, too. Lindsey, I've been waiting my whole life to find what my parents have." His expression was gentle. "I think I've found that with you."

"I love you." Saying the words felt wonderful, especially when his eyes glittered with happiness. "I was afraid to admit it, but I realized a while ago how much I loved you, Austin."

"Good. That's good." He looked a bit dazed. "Because I love you, too."

"And Josh already loves you. He's upset with me for moving us out of your house," she confided.

"Well, I can fix that." In a smooth move he swept her into his arms and carried her out the door of her tiny cottage.

"I think you're carrying me over the wrong threshold," she said with a giggle.

He gently set her on her feet outside in front of his car. "We can build a new house if you like. Something completely ours—yours, mine and Josh's."

She shook her head. His offer was generous, but there was no need. Being in love with Austin felt right. He'd already loved her longer than Sam had. And he was the kind of guy who would always work toward a better marriage. "Take me home, Austin."

"Are you sure?" he asked, giving her a chance to change her mind.

"I'm sure." She smiled. "We won't need a new house until after we've filled your bedrooms with babies."

He flashed a sexy, hopeful grin. "Sounds like an excellent plan to me."

MEDICAL™

Large Print

Titles for the next six months...

October

THE DOCTOR'S ROYAL LOVE-CHILD	Kate Hardy
HIS ISLAND BRIDE	Marion Lennox
A CONSULTANT BEYOND COMPARE	Joanna Neil
THE SURGEON BOSS'S BRIDE	Melanie Milburne
A WIFE WORTH WAITING FOR	Maggie Kingsley
DESERT PRINCE, EXPECTANT MOTHER	Olivia Gates

November

NURSE BRIDE, BAYSIDE WEDDING	Gill Sanderson
BILLIONAIRE DOCTOR, ORDINARY NURSE	Carol Marinelli
THE SHEIKH SURGEON'S BABY	Meredith Webber
THE OUTBACK DOCTOR'S SURPRISE BRIDE	Amy Andrews
A WEDDING AT LIMESTONE COAST	Lucy Clark
THE DOCTOR'S MEANT-TO-BE MARRIAGE	Janice Lynn

December

SINGLE DAD SEEKS A WIFE	Melanie Milburne
HER FOUR-YEAR BABY SECRET	Alison Roberts
COUNTRY DOCTOR, SPRING BRIDE	Abigail Gordon
MARRYING THE RUNAWAY BRIDE	Jennifer Taylor
THE MIDWIFE'S BABY	Fiona McArthur
THE FATHERHOOD MIRACLE	Margaret Barker

⊚™ MILLS & BOON®

Pure reading pleasure™

0908 LP 2P P1 Medical

MEDICAL™

Large Print

January

VIRGIN MIDWIFE, PLAYBOY DOCTOR	Margaret McDonagh
THE REBEL DOCTOR'S BRIDE	Sarah Morgan
THE SURGEON'S SECRET BABY WISH	Laura Iding
PROPOSING TO THE CHILDREN'S DOCTOR	Joanna Neil
EMERGENCY: WIFE NEEDED	Emily Forbes
ITALIAN DOCTOR, FULL-TIME FATHER	Dianne Drake

February

THEIR MIRACLE BABY	Caroline Anderson
THE CHILDREN'S DOCTOR AND THE SINGLE MUM	Lilian Darcy
THE SPANISH DOCTOR'S LOVE-CHILD	Kate Hardy
PREGNANT NURSE, NEW-FOUND FAMILY	Lynne Marshall
HER VERY SPECIAL BOSS	Anne Fraser
THE GP'S MARRIAGE WISH	Judy Campbell

March

SHEIKH SURGEON CLAIMS HIS BRIDE	Josie Metcalfe
A PROPOSAL WORTH WAITING FOR	Lilian Darcy
A DOCTOR, A NURSE: A LITTLE MIRACLE	Carol Marinelli
TOP-NOTCH SURGEON, PREGNANT NURSE	Amy Andrews
A MOTHER FOR HIS SON	Gill Sanderson
THE PLAYBOY DOCTOR'S MARRIAGE PROPOSAL	Fiona Lowe

MILLS & BOON®

Pure reading pleasure™

0908 LP 2P P2 Medical

APL		CCS	
Cen		Ear	22|10|08
Mob		Cou	
ALL		Jub	
WH		CHE	
Ald		Bel	
Fin		Fol	
Can		STO	
Til		HCL	